T0354846

S.S. SIMPSON
BROKEN

authorHOUSE

AuthorHouse™
1663 Liberty Drive
Bloomington, IN 47403
www.authorhouse.com
Phone: 1 (800) 839-8640

© 2019 S.S. Simpson. All rights reserved.

No part of this book may be reproduced, stored in a retrieval system, or transmitted by any means without the written permission of the author.

Published by AuthorHouse 12/19/2019

ISBN: 978-1-7283-4042-5 (sc)
ISBN: 978-1-7283-4041-8 (e)

Print information available on the last page.

Any people depicted in stock imagery provided by Getty Images are models, and such images are being used for illustrative purposes only.
Certain stock imagery © Getty Images.

This book is printed on acid-free paper.

Because of the dynamic nature of the Internet, any web addresses or links contained in this book may have changed since publication and may no longer be valid. The views expressed in this work are solely those of the author and do not necessarily reflect the views of the publisher, and the publisher hereby disclaims any responsibility for them.

CONTENTS

CONTENTS

To Raema, a Christian warrior who heals the broken.
Thank you for helping me polish my book.

THE BEGINNING

||||||||||||||||||||||||||||||||||||||||||||||||||||||||||||||||||||||||||||||||||||||||||||||||||||||||||||||||||||||||||||||||

The shrill ring of the phone pulled me out of my paperwork. It was the hotel operator insisting that I talk to the gentleman on the phone, since he was on my list.

"Good afternoon, this is Maggie. How may I help you?"

In the background, in between sobs, all that I could hear was a lady's high-pitched voice screaming, "I can't find it, I lost it."

"It's my wife, Sara. We just got off the plane and she can't find her passport. Sara just emptied everything out of her carry-on luggage in the middle of the floor. Security guards have cordoned us off. I'm sure they think we're terrorists or trying to do something illegal. All I see are worried faces and loaded guns on black leather belts. This is not what I expected. The brochure's instructions stated that you would meet us with your Canadian flag. Where are you?"

This had to be Dr. Angel and his wife from Texas. They were the only ones missing from my list.

"Dr. Angel, you need to calm Sara down or you may find yourself truly secluded where I can't help you. The airport security doesn't tolerate any outbursts. There's an American Embassy close by where Sara can get another passport. The important thing is that you find an airport shuttle and get to the hotel." Dr. Angel paused quietly. Then I heard, "Sir, you'll have to come with me." I was too late. My warning didn't matter now. The abrupt click of the phone rudely disconnected us. I was used to being in control. I wasn't now. This was definitely not the way to start a tour.

My tour was scheduled to depart early in the morning. There wasn't any time for delays. Worry tore at me. I would wait only one hour. Then I would take matters into my own hands. It needed to be done diplomatically.

My dues were paid in full. In the travel business, my reputation was never questioned. Dr. Angel and his wife Sara would be on my bus at seven o'clock in the morning. Within minutes, my pen, fingers, and mind were inseparable. Like runaways, my contacts raced through my mind.

"Please allow my wife to get her things back in her bag. Where are you taking us?"

"It doesn't matter. You'll find out soon enough."

"Is this really necessary? My wife lost her passport. Women get rattled. Surely you can understand that."

"You'll both be thoroughly checked." Dr. Angel knew that things couldn't get much worse. Sara's coping skills were gone. Catatonic, she followed him like a broken robot. A roped-off area was directly in front of them. Out of nowhere, solemn faces appeared.

"We're Americans on vacation. We've done nothing wrong. My wife just can't find her passport."

"Sir, I need to see your passport."

An alarm sounded as Doctor Angel fumbled for his identification. The searching wand stopped at his leg. Commotion erupted. He was grabbed by two men and taken to a cold room.

"My leg, it's a prosthesis. It has metal reinforcements."

"We have to check it. Raise your trouser leg," was all that Dr. Angel heard.

"It's attached to my stump."

"Detach it."

Dr. Angel was past embarrassment. He no longer cared what happened to him. This was harassment. He was handicapped and was very aware of his rights. He knew what they could and couldn't do.

"It is painful for me to take my leg off and put it on again." Dr. Angel didn't budge. His upper body was strong. His dignity meant more to him than this trip. If they arrested him then Sara would just have to understand. Sara, what happened to Sara? "I need to see my wife."

One of the violators quickly departed. When Sara witnessed her husband manhandled and led away, something snapped in her brain. Her fight, her teacher instinct flared and rose up like hot steam. Sara was permitted to leave the area, but wasn't going anywhere without her husband. She didn't care if the whole airport knew it and demanded that something be done. Others listened.

"You're free to go."

Dr. Angel thought that he had misunderstood. Then he heard his bewildered wife.

"It's over. We can leave."

"But I thought..." Dr. Angel didn't need an explanation. Other eyes said it all. Clutching Sara's hand, he searched for the nearest exit. "Did you ever figure out how to get to the hotel?"

"No. The phone disconnected us."

"Maggie, this is Dr. Angel. I apologize for the abrupt disconnection, but Sara and I were briefly detained. Sara still hasn't located her passport. There's one other huge problem. My luggage is missing. It contains my leg charger. Tomorrow, I won't be able to move without it."

I wasn't quite sure that I understood the doctor correctly. I knew he was exhausted but now he was bionic? Hearing that everything is bigger and better in Texas I guess it was possible.

"Dr. Angel, I'm just so glad to get your call. Your luggage will turn up. No matter what time of night it arrives, the shuttle operator will bring it to the hotel. Take a breath, get on the shuttle, and get off at the right hotel."

My mind screeched to a halt. The mystery couple was safe and headed this way. Earlier I placed welcome letters at the front desk for members of my tour when they checked in.

As their tour guide, my clients needed to know that I was in charge and that my rules applied to everyone with no exception. Western Canada awaited us. Before one foot stepped on that bus, tourists knew what to expect and what not to expect. Some choices were up to the tourists. They had to be documented.

By 7:00 tomorrow morning, my paper work needed to be flawless. The tour bus would make its way to Banff, which was about six-scenery numbing hours away. The long bus ride would not be disappointing. I knew all too well what my wide-eyed guests wanted: time to enjoy mother bears with their cubs, mammoth mountains, gushing waterfalls, and knotty pine trees, because like a fine wine, they knew their glass could be emptied at any time.

Western Canada was my personal, carved-out niche. Given the fact that I grew up in Calgary, I was very familiar with every bit of its distinctive territory. My fondest memories center around my dad and his bus; every day the two of us created an adventure for expectant tourists. Sitting right beside him, I became a permanent fixture watching, listening, and absorbing everything like a Canadian bath sponge. Even today, when I board my bus, that ten-year-old spirit takes control and Dad is right beside me.

Once in a while, certain male bus drivers get the wrong impression thinking that they are the magic. After their fantasies are correctly realigned, the real magic begins and I trigger the vacation fantasies. Buses invite possibilities, and tourists expect to see what the colorful brochure has promised regardless of unexpected circumstances.

When I was selected for this job, I will never forget the interview. It troubled the employer that I had no past counseling experience. I wasn't even a teacher. Was I able to cope with unsettling situations? I handled my father. That answered it for me. I knew firsthand that obsessed tourists were stubborn and relentless. At times, like spoiled brats. I was good at turning defiance into adherence. No matter what, the detailed itinerary always took precedence.

Looking for the shuttle, Dr. Angel felt more confident as he herded his wife towards the crowd. Watching everything, he couldn't believe all the activities. It was hectic like the university where he taught. Five years ago, he retired. What was left of his heart was still there. Six, stubborn, clogged arteries almost killed him. His aggressive, pushy professor ways never left him and he used them now. Cutting in front of the shuttle line, he started inquiring, but then heard an agitated voice holler:

"Hey, what do you think you're doing? There's a line and it's behind me."

He realized he wasn't at the university where no one dared questioned him. Feeling a cane knocking on his left calf, he turned around ready to punch. He couldn't believe his eyes. It was a little old man, about eighty-five, adorned with a stylish hat, white hair and pride, lots of it. His glaring blue eyes wouldn't let Dr. Angel look away.

"I, ah, really didn't realize that there was a line. I just need to get on this shuttle."

"So, do we."

"My wife and I have been traveling since early this morning from Texas and, well, I need to know when this shuttle leaves and where it's going."

"My wife and I have been up since predawn and have been traveling all day from California."

Dr. Angel didn't want to proceed with this conversation, so he just right-fronted himself, and got the shuttle information. The old man continued tapping on Dr. Angel's leg with his annoying cane and couldn't believe the rudeness displayed by his fellow American. He was so much younger. Where was his respect for elders?

Grabbing Sara and her overly stuffed, zipper-jammed suitcase, Dr. Angel couldn't get away from that tapping cane fast enough.

After finally locating the shuttle, the driver, and other distressed passengers, the two Texans were jammed together like squashed toes in a too-tight sneaker.

"This is the Sandyman Hotel," barked the sickly driver, coughing and sneezing for the entire thirty-minute ride. Determined not to catch any Canadian germs, Sara found a used discarded napkin in her pocket that she awkwardly breathed through. Unfortunately, her educated husband chose to sit right next to the Canadian germs and inhaled them the whole way. He could have used a Kleenex but his image meant everything to him. Sara, on the other hand, wasn't concerned about other people and their opinions.

Sara was a trapped crab in an overly snug burrow and bolted out of the van as it pulled to a stop. Patience didn't describe her, quite the opposite. Sara's tendency was to vanish. Her mother insisted that she was part Indian. Leon needed extra time and help because he had an artificial leg that seemed to have a mind of its own. Unsuspecting bystanders often ended up assisting because Sara was never there. Suddenly Sara remembered that she was part of a couple and backtracked to the van where Leon was struggling.

"Sara, could you help me with my leg? I just can't seem to get it unstuck," panicked Leon, who was holding up the other impatient passengers. They were anxiously waiting to be rid of their condemned spaces. Somehow Leon's leg was wedged in between the mat and the door, so Sara gave the leg a yank, feeling her back pinch and her mind winch.

Sara hated when people stared and by now she had their undivided attention. The driver was preoccupied, sputtering in French-Canadian sprinkled with English. After freeing his stubborn leg, Sara grabbed their only luggage bag. Digging deeply in her napkin pocket, she retrieved some American dollars and gave them to the driver. Instantly, the driver's verbal spasm stopped. Hotels usually impressed her, but this one didn't.

"Leon, we're right smack in the middle of an office complex." Observed Sara, frowning as she pulled apart the drapes. Her nonfunctioning husband redirected his gaze.

"Sara, remember we're only here for one night, actually what little is left of it," responded Leon, knowing how claustrophobic his hyper wife could become. His soothing ability evaporated with his lost luggage. Silence was all that he wanted.

Sara had to share every thought with him. A foreign country had not suppressed that whim. His worn-out nerves twitched.

"Regarding those drapes, make sure you keep them closed or you'll be the early-morning entertainment for the entire block." Sara disliked waking up to darkness, but could easily envision the early-morning gossiping secretaries as they peered into their undraped room.

"Sara, there's one more thing that needs to happen early tomorrow morning. My luggage has to get here if you want to continue as a touring couple. Unless I'm able to retrieve my leg charger and recharge my prosthesis for a significant period of time, I'll be an immovable piece of cement. You need to be ready to leave without me." He watched his horrified wife wince and turn away.

THE BUS

The shriek of the hotel's telephone made Sara squirm. It was awfully early, and the sleeping clock's hands confirmed her suspicions. This was even earlier than a regular hectic school day. Was she really on vacation? Yes she was. The heavy dark drapes stared back at her.

Leon reached for the phone, expecting the worse, but it was the best.

"Sara, my luggage was found and they're sending it right up. It will give me enough time to get my bionic status back."

Huddled way down under the covers with Leon's socks pulled up to her knees, Sara poked her head out again. An early rush of relief like whistling wind through a pine grove swept through her. She wouldn't have to make that uncomfortable decision of leaving Leon behind.

"Sara, would you really have left without me?"

She didn't answer. It was Leon's time to squirm.

"Leon, last night in the welcome letter, it stated that the bags have to be out in the hallway by six o'clock. Is that really what they expect?"

A voice outside their door confirmed it.

"Bags need to be outside in fifteen minutes or it's not going on the bus," said the hurried voice.

Leon entertained himself by watching Sara's antics. Pushing, shoving, and cramming all her things back into her suitcase wasn't easy. Sara didn't even have time for her crank-oil as her dad called it; intense strong coffee gladdened with brown sugar and cream. This was a vacation, not a job. Rules didn't belong in the Canadian Rockies.

An incessant knock tapped lightly at the door. The valet dropped off Leon's luggage and didn't leave. *We both forgot that at six o'clock in the morning, tipping was also expected.* Leon's mind whirled. Was his prosthesis

7

charger there? Would he have enough time? He groped and felt the wired plug. Exhaling a long sigh, Leon was thankful that both of them would be able to continue the expensive trip that was given as an anniversary present from his in-laws. I think it was their way of appreciation for his loving endurance.

Maggie was up early, leaving a few extra hours before departure to take care of last-minute items. Last evening, she met the designated group minus the bionic American couple. She wasn't disappointed; it was an international group. They are the best kind usually on their best behavior. No one knows what to expect when various accents flavor the air: The Scots with their slowed, refined accents are relieved to escape their moody weather. The English enunciate their syllables quite properly and enjoy gracious customs such as high tea. Weathered Hussies from New Zealand emphasize random sounds and are annoyed when others think that kangaroos live on their island, since they are found only in Australia. The Israelis with their lower-range sounds and outward kindness are grateful that they don't have to fear who is standing next to them or who might be around the corner. The Filipinos with their shrill, undulating voices are slight in stature, but make up for it in curiosity and organization. The Germans with their westernized speech, sport-pronounced mannerisms, and independent ways. But the Americans—how could she forget them: speaking a mile a minute, never pausing in their drama. Never even considering that others didn't want to listen to it.

My departure routine was automatic. Name tags were first, which needed to be placed above the seats in an orderly systematic fashion. First come, first served is not applicable on the bus. The seats were assigned so if you got to the bus an hour early, it didn't matter. If you chose to get to the bus an hour late, it did matter. It wouldn't be there. By rotation everyone would have a chance to be up front, since it was the best place to sit. Necks would twist every which way scouring for coveted bears, white-tailed mountain goats, and other Canadian heartthrobs.

Hopefully the company had selected a competent bus driver. A good sense of humor was mandatory as well as the innate ability to look like his eyes were glued to the road even if they weren't. Usually the bus drivers were interchanged with different tour guides, which kept relationships professional. In the tour business, time was money and every minute counted. My job was to keep the tour at designated stops at designated times. With an international group this size, I needed to be more than ready for anything. A tap on my shoulder jolted me out of my mental preparation.

"Excuse me, I'm looking for Maggie, our tour guide," asked a tired voice. As I turned around, a head of blonde hair and steely blue eyes grabbed my undivided attention.

"I'm Maggie, and you must be Sara from Texas. You finally made it. Your husband, is he here with you?"

"Leon is sitting down over there."

Looking in her direction, I noticed an older man who was fiddling with his watch. As he rose, he certainly didn't look bionic. In fact, he was having some trouble walking and had to stop.

"My husband can't do a great deal of walking, so I needed to ask you if we could sit up front in the bus."

"Yes, that would be a good idea." Realizing that suddenly my job had gotten tougher since having a handicapped person getting on and off the bus, procedures would be slower, more complicated. In Canada, there are no equal access laws for the handicapped so I was going to have to be creative. I never had a handicapped tourist before——older, yes; slower, yes; but not physically impaired.

On the way back to the bus, a bright grin encouraged me. It was Gus whom I had worked with before. He loaded the luggage with gusto and precision, careful not to add new scratches to old.

"Maggie, by the looks of the luggage, another group from all over?" questioned Gus.

"Yup, and we have a couple from Texas that's going to need a great deal of help I'm afraid. Have you had that double-decker breakfast of yours?"

"Don't worry. Was there ever a time when we haven't been able to accommodate each and every one of our riders? It'll just take a little more patience and cooperation from everyone. Let the Texans get on first, then off last when we get to the stops. If they need help, the other passengers will pitch in."

Gus still believed in the goodness of people. He had no ex-wife, no children, no one questioning or defying. Fifteen years ago, my own husband deserted me. No explanations, no questions, no answers. I became a master of cover-ups, raising my son and daughter who never stopped asking why. Daily, it haunted me. Dr. Angel reminded me of my ex-husband needing help yet not wanting it.

After a head count, we were off. That's when I first noticed it. A lady from Scotland was coughing continuously. She was three seats behind me, behind Dr. Angel and his wife. Germs and I were like oil and water; we didn't mix. With a job like mine, I couldn't afford to be sick or even consider it.

Instinctively Gus interrupted the mingling, reiterating his rules, especially the one about the restroom. "May I have your attention? Once you leave a bus deposit, it just grows like a bank deposit. The smell is intoxicating, pure stench. Try to use the bus's restroom only in dire emergencies." The group's reaction was quite predictable. The women hardly blinked, but the men winced, looking trapped like cornered fawns, alarmed about what they had just heard.

"Leon, don't you remember how the brochure touted the modern features on the bus, especially the fashionable, accessible restrooms, but now they have been cordoned off? What are you going to do?" asked his irritated wife.

"Sara, I'm sure that there'll be periodic stops along the way," said Leon, trying to convince himself. This certainly was not the convenience that he anticipated.

Watching the men loosen their belts, and panicking, I inhaled and slowed my best Canadian accent, wooing them.

"It should take us about thirty minutes to get to our first stop, which will be Fort Calgary, where there'll be unique presentations about Canadian history. Before we reach the fort, there are many sights that you don't want to miss. Don't forget to turn around and get the perspective from the back windows as well. You're now in Calgary, the cowboy capital of the world."

"Every year in early June, Calgary sponsors The Great Roundup which attracts cowboys and *wannabes*. Look at those enormous arenas. They're being converted into rodeo-type corals where cowboys ride bareback, lasso, rope, and tie. During this time of year, mostly everyone absorbs the cowboy lifestyle. Employers allow their workers to dress in cowboy garb, authentic pants and skirts with spurred boots. Companies and stores are decorated with hats, boots, lassos, and spurs. If you look closely on some of the lawns, you can even spot unusual cowboy sculptures. The mania never really ends."

Sara watched, fixated, thankful that she was not a cowboy. Stretched out buildings overshadowed the festival.

"Leon, I had no idea that Canada was so, well, so modern. I mean it looks just like the United States."

"Yes, and, Sara, over there, there's even a college. Can you imagine, a university, the University of Calgary? Canadians also believe in education," responded Leon, amazed sometimes at what Sara didn't know.

"This reminds me so much of Austin, Texas, where I got my doctorate in education. Notice how all the roads are wrapped around the college with its housing, restaurants, and entertainment."

Sara knew Leon was trying to tease her, but she didn't care. His intended remark flew by her like a gush of chilly wind. Leon didn't usually share how he felt, unless prodded like coals in a fire. Sara usually prodded but this morning she didn't. Her thoughts were centered on Canada, its people, customs, and the other bus passengers.

High- and low-pitched voices encircled Sara, as individuals exclaimed in their own languages. Sara's mind opened. There were possibilities, choices, and sheer enjoyment. Her obsessive concerns about how to become a better seventh grade reading teacher stopped. There were no seventh graders here. She was on vacation. Her normal routines and reactions were deafened. Leon's detached distance suddenly didn't matter.

As I answered various questions about this and that, I noticed how some of the passengers had snuggled in, especially the ones directly behind me. This particular couple was young, in love, and keenly aware of one another. Being from Israel, their rich, blackish hair and flashing auburn eyes set them apart. They delighted in one another. It was intoxicating, so polite, so concerned, so adoring. What happens to all that love as time progresses? I didn't know.

As I stared, I couldn't help but notice that Dr. Angel's wife couldn't take her eyes off the couple either. But her eyes told much more than any lovers could––a covered sadness mixed with longing. Quickly I looked away not wanting to intrude. My own emptiness devoured me.

THE UNFORGIVING FIELD

||||||||||||||||||||||||||||||||||||||||||||||||||||||||||||||||||||||||||||||||||||||||||||||||||||||||||||||||||||||||||||||||||||

D r. Angel could barely make it off the bus. Fort Calgary was a flashing neon sign of what was to come. His young wife couldn't wait to get off the bus, and left him a few steps behind, well, out of sight.

Spying the stone benches in the courtyard's entrance, Dr. Angel decided to rest while checking his bionic parts, making sure they were all still attached. The lurches on the bus were unexpected. Maybe Gus had a heavy foot or maybe he needed to make one of those bank deposits.

I couldn't help but notice how much trouble Dr. Angel had in just getting off the bus even though he waited until the bus emptied. Hardly able to maneuver the steps, he barely made it to the scenic viewing area and collapsed. His eager wife had rushed ahead, disappearing, where she was abruptly captivated by our Royal Canadian Mounted Police. I sensed her fascination. Our "Mounties" were walking time capsules.

Once inside Fort Calgary, one was drawn back to the 1800s when law and order was secured by these regal-looking men. Donned in their red coats with embossed gold buttons, white gloves, long brown boots, and brown hats, the Mounties convinced you to be on the lookout for alarming Indian behavior in this raw Western Canadian wilderness.

Our Canadian history was so diverse: courageous women trailblazing over the Rockies alongside Chinese immigrants, who were paid almost nothing as they connected the territories with the Continental Railroad. Visitors always seemed so amazed that we even have a history, especially the Americans, and Sara was no exception.

Yanked out of her absorption, Sara realized that she had forgotten about Leon. Frantically looking from room to room, she spied him on the outside benches and hurried over.

"Why didn't you wait for me? You know that I'm hurting. Sara, I need your help." Leon breathed with difficulty, unable to catch his breath. He knew that he was in trouble. This was the first day, the first stop, and he could hardly move. His cane didn't seem to help at all; he might as well be using a stick. Sara needed to know that she was going to have to slow down and not leave his side.

"I know, I should have waited for you, but I couldn't. I just needed to get off that bus and move my legs."

Still filled with Monty museum glow, Sara added, "I never realized that Canada had the same kind of developmental problems that we had in the United States. They had a railroad; you know, just like we did. Their county's history is really just an extension of what happened to us: the settlers, the Indians, the lawlessness."

"Sara, right now you need to concentrate on me or you'll have to absorb all this wonderful history by yourself. I just don't think I can do this."

Immediately, Sara switched modes, from adventurous, to automatic, giving her undivided attention to her ailing husband. As she accepted his full weight on her frail body frame, her back screamed in protest.

The next two hours passed. This time it was Sara's turn to hurt. Since the museum there had been no stops. While Leon napped and breathed, Sara twisted and turned, checking the views from each window, not wanting to miss a single detail. She was more than ready for another stop. The creeping motion sickness had reawakened her hatred of buses, which lay tucked under many layers of time.

She was once again that awkward seventh grader. Because of the distance junior high school meant taking the bus. Once you got on the bus, no one ever wanted to share their seat. In order to sit down, she had to push the other kid's stuff out of the way. It made her feel like an unwanted virus. But getting the seat wasn't the worst part. With each abrupt stop and start, the headaches and nausea swept through her body. So she came up with an ingenious plan.

Tricking the sickness, she got off the bus at her elementary school, which allowed her a two-mile walk to recover before reaching school. It worked brilliantly, but there was a drawback. Her peers made fun of her since they assumed that she didn't know that she was no longer in elementary school. Since no one could figure her out, she was labeled and became an outcast. Because no one dared talk to her, there wasn't even a slight possibility of making friends.

Her well-meaning mother insisted that she have friends, so the ritual of Friday afternoon buddy bribery began. With the promise of countless snacks, the chance to climb her backyard cliff, and the opportunity to talk to her handsome brother, she got volunteers. Her mother thought she was popular, her brother enjoyed the admiration and giggling stares, and everyone was happy, except Sara. One cover-up led to another, until her lies became her reality. Her mother only wanted her to be accepted, to fit in with the others, but she never did. To this day, she was still very self-conscious around people she didn't know...like the ones on this bus.

"Leon, I don't think the lady behind me on the bus likes me." Leon couldn't believe what he heard.

"Sara, she doesn't even know you," Leon answered, knowing Sara was insecure but this was ridiculous.

"You know how I like to watch everything from all different directions. Well, every time I turned around looking at things through the back windows, the lady behind me asked her husband if I annoyed him."

"Well, did you?"

"No, he said that I didn't. But then his wife said that she wanted to change their seat."

"Sara, you just like to jump around a lot, quite a lot, most people don't. So just forget it and maybe the lady will absorb some of your energy, who knows. Concentrate on that, over there," prompted Leon, as the vertical mountain swayed its gondola.

"Now, you'll be able to absorb all the scenery that you can hold, fidgeting to your heart's content. After we get off the bus, I need to make a bank deposit, and warm up a bit in the chalet."

"On your left is Sulphur Mountain named after the super hot springs that three men stumbled upon," offered Maggie. "This discovery led to the establishment of Banff National Park."

Looking at their faces, I knew that they wanted to experience it by foot, not by ear. Later I could fill in the historical tidbits when their feet were exhausted.

The group couldn't get off the bus fast enough. I was awestruck by the mountain's numbing beauty. It wouldn't matter if it were the first or hundredth time. Humbled to be included in this moving portrait, I was determined to make this the best tour yet.

Following my own instructions, I headed towards the chalet as a misting dew filtered downward like sifted flour settling on outstretched boughs of pine, spruce, and jasmine. I hesitated. Taking a group up a mountain, particularly this mountain in the rain, just didn't work. When a view is stolen, tempers flare. On my evaluation form, I didn't want any cryptic remarks blaming me for the weather, which most tourists assumed that I controlled.

Olaf, a surprised Swede interrupted my doubts.

"That mountain sure doesn't compare to the Alps. Sulphur Mountain appears gentle, small, snowless, and accessible."

I guess it was all a matter of perspective, but right now I needed a clear one. Then as if someone flipped a switch, the sifting stopped. Eager tourists clamored for their options. Some of the Swiss and Austrians chose the walking trails. They were visual posters. Others opted for an easier climb, the gondola, which promised a more relaxing panoramic view. The chalet enticed a different crowd. A mug of hot cocoa loaded with bobbing marshmallows and whipped cream could warm the coldest thoughts.

For me, this three-hour respite meant additional time to verify our accommodations for tonight, ensuring that everyone who requested accessibility in the hotel received it. Dr. Angel and his wife were definitely on my mind as I couldn't help but overhear their concerned conversation.

"Sara, you'd never know that you're an avid snow skier, conquering Vail, and Sun Valley in Utah. Why are you so hesitant?"

"This is different. There isn't any snow. With snow, everything blends together masking the height perspective. But look at that slope, it's all rocks and trails going straight up."

"When we get to the gondola just sit on the side facing down the mountain. You won't even notice the altitude."

Being persuasive seemed to be one of Dr. Angel's natural traits. I watched the slow-moving couple make their way towards the lift-line.

As usual, Leon was right and before Sara knew it, they were both strapped into the gondola as it climbed vertically, effortlessly, silently up the mountain. Leon sparkled with "oohs and aahs." Aiming her camera at Leon, Sara hoped to capture his amazement. She zoomed in on his unusual carefree grin and clicked, but nothing happened; the battery was completely dead.

"Of course the camera doesn't work, why would it?" Pouted Sara, frustrated knowing she should have checked it.

"Sara, don't get agitated. Once we reach the top, there should be a place where you can buy some batteries," Leon replied. But the moment was gone, that grin, that electric grin vanished. Sara wished she planned ahead, like Leon. But she was spontaneous and never gave a thought about the tomorrows. Leon was consumed by tomorrows. Sadly, he never knew how to enjoy the todays. But if he had his camera, it would be working.

As the gliding gondola neared the dismounting station, Sara watched the confident faces of those helping. As the doors opened, guiding hands and arms reached in while Leon's and Sara's arms reached out. Suddenly, the doors started moving with Leon stuck in the middle. Sara pulled Leon towards her toppling backwards. The motor suddenly shut down, halting the lift completely. The jammed doors opened, discarding Leon like tasteless wine. Red-faced and breathless, Leon stumbled, reaching for Sara. He hadn't planned on a squeezing match at the top of the mountain. He was completely drained.

"Sara, I can't go on, I have to sit down. That's why I hate getting on and off moving things. Did you see what happened? The doors had me in their vicelike grip. They wouldn't let me go. My legs wouldn't move." Questioning eyes fastened on Leon. Sara knew how much he hated the stares, the pity. It was now her turn to reassure him.

"It could have happened to anyone. You were just in the right place at the wrong time. With mechanical devices, things happen," Sara quipped, trying to convince herself that it was just a slight malfunction, completely unaware of how serious it would turn out to be.

Straight ahead, there was a chimney bellowing smoke, puffing with ease. The chalet was a relative of the lower chalet, yet smaller, less accessible.

Settled and with a window view, Leon carefully sipped steaming soup. Sara was more than ready for her private adventure. She couldn't imagine staying inside while there was so much outside. People took so much for granted. She didn't. Not one detail escaped her attention. The trails called to her, but so did Leon.

"No disappearing act, Sara, keep track of the time. We have to be back on the bus in three hours." Leon knew that his wife had to be part Apache, vanishing at any given moment, day or night. Now he could relax since the chair underneath him behaved.

As if on cue, Sara clamored up the winding steps to one of the lookout towers. Noticing imprints of various animals and birds etched in the dirt, she hesitated as her New England eyes couldn't get enough of the mountains that embraced her. Living in Texas for the last twenty years seemed like a life sentence. She had agreed to move to be near her parents. Yet, her heart and soul never stopped longing for Connecticut, its hills, its seasons––the autumn leaves that dripped in scarlet reds, muted oranges, and brilliant yellows. The wintry, silver birches that rocked to and fro in the wind, glistening, drenched with icicles, as snowcapped roofs and trees bowed with their extra white load. Spring tulips in manicured rows of reds, whites, pinks, and yellows adorned thawed-out gardens. Pink and white, lacey dogwoods perfumed the air with their intoxicating blossoms. Rocky beaches loaded with smelly, popping seaweed meant summertime. Hidden coves made perfect swimming holes and a chance to see passing sailboats looking for the perfect wind, postcard material. Then there was Texas, hot, dry, and flat. She tolerated it. She hated it.

Leon loved watching Sara watch. It was better than any movie. Her love for the outdoors continually surprised him. He often kidded Sara about pitching a tent in the backyard so that she could sleep outside. Nature and her cats were her first loves. Maybe he was a close second. At times he wondered why she cared for him at all. Being handicapped, and having difficulty walking was not exactly what an active, carefree person like Sara needed. He tried to convince her of that before he married her, but she wouldn't listen. Now she listened and he felt guilty.

It was a productive afternoon. As a relaxed tour guide I let my guard down, watching exhausted, yet content shapes fill the chalet. Hands grabbed for pocket memories wanting to take a part of the mountain with them. It was a good sign for the first outing with the local economy benefiting as well. Giving back was something that my father instilled in me. Nothing mattered more than the land. Our national parks needed to be preserved. Tourists did that. Suddenly, as if by instinct, they headed for the bus, a swarm of bees to a hive. I didn't need to check my watch.

Gus's sit-up nap ended abruptly, as he welcomed the swarm, helping them reboard. It was reassuring to know Gus was there. If something unexpected were to happen, I knew that there were two extra hands to help me.

Counting and recounting, my head count was off by four people. It shouldn't be since it was ten minutes past departure time. It was the doctor and his wife from Texas and the elderly couple from California, two couples that shouldn't be missing. Dr. Angel, a retired professor was very time-oriented and the California couple made it a point to inform other passengers how the time zones functioned in the United States. So how could two time-educated couples be unaccountable? My stomach turned, my quiet repose vanished.

Meanwhile, Sara and Leon, who were bracing for another door attack, waited for the rounding gondola. Just as the gondola came into view, Sara heard a spunky voice, "May we join you?" It was getting late and cold, so Sara reluctantly made room for the tired couple. After all, she had enjoyed a completely selfish afternoon walking many uplifting trails, climbing up jagged rocks, and wondering how things might be different.

Leon seemed pleased, welcoming the strangers. He loved meeting new people. It was Sara's worst nightmare. Studying the husband and wife, she couldn't believe her eyes. It was the agitated lady who sat behind her and her non-agitated husband. But as she looked into his pale blue Swedish eyes, she knew those eyes––and his cane. He was the elderly man at the airport who caned Leon because he rudely cut in line, like one of her impatient seventh graders. How embarrassing. *But why was he without his cane? How in the world did he get up here?* In the worst way, she wanted to ask him. Sara pulled her sweater up to her chin and was so thankful not to be recognized.

"We're from California," Dotty proclaimed, wearing a multicolored coordinated outfit with flashy jewelry. The cane hitter was less colorful, blending in with his worn blue jeans and muted-green sweat shirt. Immediately Sara liked him. Ariel's softness glowed and was nothing at all like that irate, well-aimed man with his flying cane. Leon saturated their ears with charm, easily capturing Ariel and Dotty.

In the worst way, Dotty wanted to impress the professor and his wife, the energetic twister. When Dotty learned that Sara was a teacher, she completely understood her energy level. It was a professional requirement.

"Have you noticed that we're the last ones going down the mountain? All the gondolas are empty except ours. Even the lift attendants scooted down on that all-terrain snowcat."

From the moment Dotty sat down, Sara knew that Dotty needed to talk, so she forced herself to respond.

"You're very observant. I didn't notice the other empty gondolas. On the top of the mountain with all the sun's reflection, time can be deceiving. I'm sure that others will be late as well, I can just hear Maggie now: 'As a subtle reminder, those of you who are late will have to sit in the back of the bus,' punishing us as if we were seventh graders." Sara laughed in spite of herself.

"Since this great view may be one of your last, Sara, you better inhale it," added Leon, knowing that his wife would never survive the back of the bus, nothing to see except straining necks and heads.

Ariel's eyes twinkled. "Not to worry, Maggie will empathize with me, my limitations, and my over-ninety status." Suddenly, excuses didn't matter as a grinding screech halted the gondola. It remained curiously silent minutes passed.

"This happens often with mechanical lifts," commented Sara, remembering a chairlift breakdown when skiing with her dad in snow-ambushed Vermont.

"I was on a ski lift once and it just stopped. The lift attendants couldn't restart the motor, so huge adjustable ladders hoisted stranded skiers down one by one. It was an open chairlift, freezing cold and frostbite was a major concern. Timing was critical." Watching Dotty twitch slightly, Sara realized that she was not calming anyone, quite the opposite. Leon's mantra, *think before you speak*, rang in her ears.

"But this gondola glides up and down this mountain all year long and is serviced regularly. Second, it isn't winter and we're enclosed. Third, I'm..."

"Sara, we don't need a lecture; we're not your students," Leon halfheartedly replied, bothered that Sara always felt like she had to tell everyone what to do, including him.

Ariel busted in. "Farming has taught me and Dotty a lot of patience. Mechanical problems work themselves out but in their own time." Ariel thoroughly enjoyed Sara's positive nature and her husband's inability to deal with it. Minutes passed, and the wind picked up. The swinging gondola was a conductor's wand.

"At least it has good rhythm," said Dotty, examining her jewelry, wishing she had worn her silver rings instead of the gold.

Leon was not keen on the swinging.

"Well, I don't see any ladders. Actually I don't see anything. There wasn't a single soul on this mountain, nothing moving except us."

Leon was a leader, a doer, used to making decisions for other people.

"Look around for any kind of rope or something that will hang down," Leon instructed as eyes widened, except for Sara's who was ready for a vacation adventure. In her wildest dreams, she couldn't have thought this one up.

"Maybe we could tie our jackets together, making a makeshift ladder and lower ourselves down," suggested Sara, thinking it just might work.

"Sara, that's a classic suggestion, but it isn't going to work here. Look how high we are from the ground. These are the Rocky Mountains, not Vermont's foothills. No, we have to use some kind of a rope. I think the doors will cooperate if we can just pry them open, jamming them, then swinging the gondola to that pine's top that's right beneath us."

"What about this?" Ariel's roaming eye spied some leftover rope someone had carelessly tossed underneath the seats.

Dotty's joints seemed frozen. She was no longer concerned about her fingers, but about her knees. Her rheumatoid arthritis had flared up. Knowing what that meant, she forced herself to get up and slowly move. Before Sara could help her, Ariel's fingers were hard at work kneading his wife's knees.

"My wife and I work well as a team. I know when she's hurting and she knows when I should be hurting because of my heart condition."

Sara hoped Leon heard the team part, but he wasn't listening. Leon was busy examining the rope that Ariel had uncovered, getting ready to implement his plan.

Leon quipped, "When we get off this mountain, we had better get a major refund for this 'spectacular ride,'" as he grappled with the rope redirecting his frustration, not wanting to annoy anyone with other chosen words.

"And a free dinner," added Ariel who was accustomed to uncertainty being a farmer. Yet, this was so much more, an outdoor survivor thriller and he was right in the middle of it.

"Dotty, sit here. Maybe this side will be better for your knees," Sara said, thankful that both of her knees bent. Helping the others became her priority. Sara's strenuous, daily early-morning workout routine now seemed more like a blessing than a curse.

Aided by Leon's directives, Ariel's roughened hands loosened the latch, wedging the doors open with the rope. But once the rope was anchored in place, the directives stopped. Leon wasn't at all sure what to do next. The gondola cooperated. They were in drop-down position.

Ariel volunteered to go first. Fifty years of four o'clock mornings had toughened his brain as well as his skin.

"Hold the rope steady while I try to land on that branch over there, pointing to a balsam pine limb just waiting to assist. Slowly, the calloused, weathered hands lowered themselves, as his swinging torso steadied itself landing on the limb. Amazed that he made it, Ariel realized that he might easily become the star of this thriller.

As Dotty peered down, she knew that lowering herself would require some careful maneuvering and a good deal of luck. Forcing herself past the pain, Dotty focused on her teammate's outstretched arms. In fifty years, he had never let her down, he couldn't now. Leon marveled at the acrobatic show knowing it was his turn to perform. His leg wasn't cooperating. It had a mind of its own.

"Sara, this is just not going to work. There's no way that I'm going to be able to get down that rope. You go on without me. I'll just wait up here."

"I can get you down, I know that I can. Just trust me for once in your life. There's no hidden agenda. Your ex-wife isn't here, and I'm not leaving you behind," Sara erupted. When she was determined to do something, she did it. Leon respected this endearing quality, but he never told Sara.

Every Sunday afternoon, like clockwork, Sara would practice her piano for hours, the same ten sonatas, in the same order, with the same intensity. Genetically driven, Sara wanted in the worst way to aspire, and carry on the family tradition of being able to memorize selections of music. Her grandmother was an accomplished pianist who could play anything and everything by ear. It troubled her that Sara couldn't master the technique. After thirty years, Sara was still trying.

Leon needed some of grandmother's heavenly inspiration. Somehow with Sara's help, he managed to get his footing as he dangled down the rope, connecting with the pine limb. Since his prosthesis usually detached itself on purpose, Leon was utterly amazed that he and his leg were still connected.

Sara was the finale, scampering down the rope like a caged monkey. When she was ten years old, climbing trees took up most of her time. Like riding a bike, getting back in a tree was second nature to her.

Once all four pairs of feet landed firmly on the ground, four pairs of thankful eyes peered up at the hanging rope. They had beaten the odds implementing their gymnastic extravaganza. Not wanting to forget a single bit, Ariel forced every minute detail into his mind. He couldn't wait to retell all this to his grandchildren although they probably wouldn't believe a word of it. Who would? Definitely not the impatient tourists back on the bus.

"Gus, there's something wrong, I feel it. It just doesn't add up. Those missing are very responsible. Sara and Leon are both educators. They eat and breathe reliability. Ariel and Dotty, have toured up, down, and across many countries. Being on time is not new to them. Put on one of the Lucille Ball tapes, and entertain our group with your antics until I return. Allow them to go back and forth to the chalet if they request. Fill in the missing blanks anyway that you want."

As I quickly departed the bus, I heard a throat clearing behind me. It was Gerard.

"I've been watching since I do that for a living. I'm also a number man, and know that four individuals have not returned to the bus. Of those four, I've become acquainted with two and am very aware of their physical limitations. Let me help."

I wondered what he did for a living. There was no time to figure it out.

"You're correct, two couples are not accounted for, although I'm sure they're probably huddled in the chalet enjoying a cup of steaming hot chocolate and time just got away from them."

"Not to be contradictive, but the two people that I mentioned are very tour savvy, having traveled by bus many times before. Actually they're advising me what and what not to expect on this trip," piped the Washington enigma.

Did he have to be so blunt? I refused to allow Gerard to know how frantic I was. How long did he watch and just what did he watch? He was way too proper and well-mannered, maybe a bit overdressed for a bus tour, but very articulate and one step ahead of me. I needed to pass him.

"Gerard, here's the plan: You go check out the chalet, and I'll check the more obscure places that might have delayed them."

We synchronized his Washington Rolex and my Canadian Timex, and agreed to meet back at the gondola in fifteen minutes. Following orders instantly and abruptly, he disappeared. He had done this before. His adrenaline gave him away. Needing to find my missing people, I redirected all my frantic energy.

They were the longest fifteen minutes of my life. No one had seen anyone fitting the description because most tourists blended in with one another like white shirts in a closet. Gerard came back empty-handed as well and didn't act at all surprised when he saw me.

"Did you really think we'd locate them?" he asked pointedly.

Whether or not I did, I wasn't going to give him the satisfaction by answering.

"We need to climb the mountain, up the north trail. Maybe their legs gave way and someone just couldn't make it back to the lift."

Continuing to quiz me, he asked, "Did you check with the lift operator? Are you certain that everyone got off the lift?"

"Yes, the lift shut down after the last gondola was emptied. Everyone should be off the mountain by now, all our foot hikers returned."

"Yes, but what if for some reason or other they missed the last gondola and had no choice but to hike down? Things don't always appear what they seem to be." My mind was now fully open like a raised window shade.

Gerard and I headed up the north trail. It was late in the day and shadows gave a different shape and color to things. As we trudged along, boulders that ordinarily looked harmless took on a menacing appearance. I fully expected them to detach themselves and block our way. The mountain held a secret and didn't want it known.

"Weren't you telling us on the bus that this is the season for mating brown bears and to be on the lookout for them?"

"Yes, the tourist needs something to look forward to seeing. Everyone wants to tell someone that they've seen a brown bear. Better yet, with cubs. But the reality of seeing one is usually slim unless it's a lucky sighting. Usually the brown bears prefer the wooded areas near the streams, which is quite a ways from the designated trails. Hikers would be in danger if that were not the case."

"But there are exceptions?"

Gerard didn't need an answer.

Way up ahead, the four gondola survivors were contemplating their next action shot for the thriller. Sizing up the condition of the group, Leon hoped that each of them had a guardian angel who was on red alert. To get down this mountain, they were going to need every bit of help in whatever form it came from.

Sara locked on to Leon's observing eyes and held them for a moment. He gave her that look, the one that permitted her to take charge. Well, after all she was the only one who had full capacity of her parts. Her knees were well-lubricated; she had two legs and a healthy heart. One way or the other, Sara was the one who needed to get them down the mountain. Sara welcomed the challenge.

Sara arranged them in a line like a duck with her chicks. Sara was first followed by shaky kneed Dotty, then her early-morning conditioned husband Ariel, with Leon bringing up the rear. Devouring a chocolate chip cookie that he had saved from lunch, Leon forgot about his pain. But something else wanted that cookie.

As an unfamiliar sound repeated itself, Sara instinctively cocked her head. That's when she saw it: a brown mother bear and its cub. Instantly dropping to the ground, Sara signaled the others to do the same. But Leon munched on unaware of the oncoming danger. When he saw his lined companions hunched down on the grass, he just thought that Dotty's knees and Ariel's heart needed a rest. But Sara was down as well, and she never needed to stop. Then he saw it.

Sunlight streamed through its reddish brown hair as the contented mother bear frolicked with her younger look-a-like, her adoring, adventurous cub. The cub had its nose up in the air as though he captured a particular scent, a chocolate scent. He saw it and wanted it. Carelessly, the determined cub meandered toward Leon who couldn't get the other cookie unwrapped quickly enough. Grabbing it, he threw it in the opposite direction as the curious cub scampered after it. But this was not a feeding zoo. The mother reacted in her protective mode. Rearing high on her hind legs, she opened her mouth as a hideous primal sound echoed through the mountain's silence.

Leon froze. He was unaccustomed to being bear meat. Ariel snapped into red alert. If Leon were to get down this mountain with any appendages intact, he needed to create a diversion. Ariel started to rustle the high grasses around him hoping to get the mother bear's attention. It worked too well. The mother bear didn't like her audience, three pairs of terrified eyes. But her audience quickly vanished as three pairs of flying legs headed for a nearby balsam pine. Outstretched arms flung themselves for reachable limbs lifting themselves up instead of down. Sara grabbed this way and that hoisting Ariel and Dotty up to temporary safety.

Peering out of her perch, Sara searched for Leon but saw nothing. Leon had barely escaped becoming an afternoon snack. National Geographic bear behavior episodes surged through his brain. Appearing dead was his best chance of surviving so he did it. Managing to drag himself next to a huge boulder, Leon covered himself with dead branches and grasses that he frantically pulled around him. He was as near dead as he could be waiting for the bear's grip to finalize it.

The mother bear was doing her best to pull down members of her audience, but then heard an unnerving yelp from her cub. He was entangled in some debris and couldn't free himself. Her mission was aborted as she redirected herself towards her wailing cub.

&0CR

The sun was getting lower in the sky, the air colder. I was keenly aware that if we didn't find the missing four before the sun left the sky, a night on the mountain might prove unforgiving.

"Did you hear that?" asked Gerard as his pinned-back Washington ears vibrated with the eerie bellow.

"Of course I heard it," and wished I hadn't. It was a bear's howl in verbal attack mode. The fact that I said it sent shivers up my spin.

Gerard sensed the urgency in my step and picked up the pace. Our instincts needed no collaboration. My nose was like a bloodhound's. I could smell the bear. My eyes needed to catch up.

Straight ahead, we entered a staged reenactment. Simultaneously, Gerard and I hit the dirt. Further down the path perched in a tree like frightened kittens were three desperate faces fastened to limp arms and legs. But where was the other? About forty yards ahead of me, my answer lay in a heaving mound of debris.

Off to the side there was an agitated mother bear that was trying to free her entangled cub from a patch of briar bushes. Gerard drew strategic arrows in the dirt. But this was my arena. Drawing a line through his detailed diagram, I motioned Gerard to just stay put. Circling around to the left, I hoped to blend in and free the tree-bound prisoners. I wasn't spotted but the moving mound wasn't so lucky. The untangled cub jumped on it thinking it was just for him. Not wanting another crisis, the mother bear followed, sniffed, reached down, and swiped. A stench of ripped plastic filled the air.

Gerard knew that staying put was not an option. Maggie didn't have eyes in the back of her head. Right now she needed them. Gerard heaved a rock towards his target, the mound. That did it. The mother had reached her limitations. Shoving her cub off the mound, she picked him up in her mouth and carried him away from the frustrating field heading for the downhill stream.

Immediately Gerard moved stealthily towards the mound, he smelled raw plastic and heard muffled moans. Slowly swopping his own arm under the debris, Gerard peered at a pair of terrorized eyes on an exhausted, thankful face. They were Leon's. "Your pant leg is torn through but there isn't any blood. You should be bleeding profusely." Gerard thought he was hallucinating. Checking the other leg, he became even more confused.

There were no visible rips or tears anywhere. Gerard was unaccustomed to being confused. Feeling uneasy and out of control, he knew that none of it made any sense.

"I don't have a leg. It's prosthesis. Sara, where's Sara? You have to find her—the others," whispered Leon, unable to hold on any longer. Closing his eyes, he reached for his real leg and then blacked out.

Finally I reached Sara and the others.

"It's Leon, go back, the mound," shrieked Sara as her eyes popped and uncontrolled tears swarmed down her face like bees on a hive. "My husband, the bear," Sara's branch snapped.

In a trancelike state, two other pairs of eyes stared back at me. They were exhausted, lost and terrified. I needed to calm them down immediately. Sara was in emotional shock, Dotty knee-shocked, and Ariel just wanted to end the desperate adventure.

Sitting up, Sara examined the battleground, and, from a distance, saw Leon twisted on the ground. Her worst thoughts were confirmed. Every minute counted. Sara had to get to him; he had to know. Barreling across the unforgiving field, she reached him, pulled him to her and listened, listened for anything. Then she heard it.

"Your husband's going to be okay. He just had an untimely encounter with a protective mother bear. His prosthesis was torn, but the rest of him was left untouched. He blacked out momentarily, but he'll be good as new once we get him off this mountain," stated Gerard no longer baffled.

Sara couldn't believe that Gerard was standing right behind her, and witnessed the entire episode. How in the world did he get here so quickly? She didn't care. She just wanted him to go away. This was her husband and wanted to be alone with him. As Sara caressed Leon, she pressed her shaking hand on his forehead urging him to come back to her. Remembering that Leon toted a water bottle, Sara fumbled for it, drenching Leon's pale face and parched throat.

"Leon, please don't leave me. I need you. I know that everything I do upsets you, but I will try harder. I will." Slowly, Leon's sealed eyes opened.

"Sara, it didn't get me. It got it," pointing to his fake leg. His weary eyes closed again but now she was here, now she was safe and she knew. As Maggie and the others hobbled towards them, Sara suddenly realized that her mental drama was over. She no longer needed to be responsible, in charge. As every ounce of inner strength vanished, Sara collapsed, wrapping Leon's lifeless arms around her.

Dotty saw the collapsed pair and joined them. Her knees were red, swollen, and inflamed. Ariel witnessed Dotty's limits hours ago. Ariel's heart burst with farmer pride. Dotty proved herself, reacting like a farmer's wife, beating the elements. Ariel vowed never again to harass Dotty about balancing the checkbook and spending money they didn't have. Ariel no longer cared; she was entitled to every bit of it.

Looking at the emotional and physical carnage sprawled around me, I grabbed my cell phone and dialed. There was no more time to waste on this obstacle course. Gerard ardently listened while Ariel supplied the missing details about the rest of the afternoon.

At last, mechanical shrieks filled the air; as all-terrain vehicle (ATVs) roared into view. The dismounting attendants couldn't quite believe their unprepared eyes. First and foremost, the gondola had closed hours ago. Secondly, why were these tourists up here with their well-accomplished tour guide? They recognized Maggie who was anything but a novice. Their silent questions went unanswered.

The attendants carefully hoisted Dotty and Leon to padded, secured seats behind mounted drivers. Once the human cargo was loaded, the vehicles sauntered off, knowing a non-bumpy ride was imperative. Sara chose to walk. Ariel, Gerard, and I followed as if in a silent procession down the mountain.

Gus had entertained the awaiting passengers with numerous tapes, free coupons for just about anything in the chalet and many excuses, most of which made absolutely no sense. As Maggie's face came into view, he was a kid in a shopping mall that had just been found.

Feeling very relieved, Gus knew that his solo show was over. But his relief subsided when he saw the held-up figure behind Maggie. Leon was propped up, a mangled puppet between two attendants. His pant leg was ripped, and he stumbled as his pale face was shrouded in pain. Following Leon was another escorted figure, a red-faced female who could barely walk. He thought it was Dotty but her voice was oddly silent. Behind her were three unescorted figures whose faces were drawn, exhausted, and expressionless. Gus recognized Sara, the professor's wife, since she usually clamored over her husband on the bus seat. The other was the elderly

California farmer and that determined passenger, Gerard, who bounded off the bus aiding Maggie on her quest.

Immediately, other passengers' personal issues faded as the missing four boarded the bus. Bobbing heads strained while arms and legs moved quickly making ample room for the newly arrived.

"Gus, I need you to get us to the inn as competently as possible. No jolts, no deer veering, no chances, okay?"

I didn't give him time to answer. Volunteered empty drink containers still chunked with melting ice were passed to the back of the bus. While elevating her legs, Ariel constructed crude ice packs for Dotty's knees. He was well-versed in taking care of her knees usually using a wastebasket stuffed with ice.

"Leon, I know how much you loathe your prosthesis, but I'll be forever indebted to it—for saving your life," Sara lovingly rambled just wanting her husband to feel secure. Sara was still afraid of what didn't happen. Leon considered what Sara just said.

Once the embossed paw print of the bear was removed from his mind, he would make a conscious effort not to curse at his prosthesis when it pinched, tugged, or fell off his agitated stump.

As the bus pulled away, I couldn't help but notice the relieved looks on the attendant's faces. They couldn't wait to see us depart, the quicker the better. Publicity like this was deadly for all involved. The gondoliers would have their day of reckoning as soon as I submitted a well-documented report with Ariel's help who now looked as though he were rethinking his life's vocation and becoming a film director.

A SCOTTISH KILT

||||||||||||||||||||||||||||||||||||||||||||||||||||||||||||||||||||||||||||||||||||||||||||||||||||||||||||||||||||||||||||

T hankful that there was only one scheduled gondola ride for this tour, I slowly unwound. No shrieking sirens woke me during the night. I assumed both patients were mending as both Dotty and the professor declined professional medical attention.

A free day in Banff was just what any doctor would have ordered for any person on that bus especially after yesterday's calamity. The Canadian Rockies could soften any circumstance as they unwrapped their numbing charm around those who ventured down their winding roads. Uncertainty didn't belong here. A cleared mind did. After anticipating the needs and wants of a busload of clamoring tourists, all that I wanted was some of that clearness, some alone time or so I thought.

Throughout the night, Sara vigilantly watched Leon for at least an hour until he breathed quietly. Getting Leon's agreeing nod, today was her day. There were no five o'clock wake-up calls, no frantic-packing war cries, no suitcases thrown outside in the hallway by six thirty, and no stuffing herself in a cramped bus seat beside her fairly relaxed husband. The gondola-free mountains beckoned her.

Sara usually did her exploring without Leon and today was no exception, wondering how to get to The Fairmont Hotel. Sara couldn't wait to see its gallantry since its reputation preceded it. Yesterday, Maggie impressed the group with the history of this Canadian wonder. A map was all that Sara needed showing bus routes and access points, straight ahead stood her answer.

"Maggie, I wanted to know the best way to get to that renowned hotel. The one that was first built backwards, having the extravagant guest rooms facing the woods with the kitchen and employee's quarters facing the beautiful Bow Valley."

My alone time just vanished. That look in Sara's eyes worried me. I didn't need another missing tourist. Sara needed an escort and found one.

"Sara, I was going to head up that way myself, but what about Leon?" I queried not really understanding how she could leave him alone after yesterday's close call. If Leon were my husband I wouldn't leave him for a second especially to go see a hotel regardless of its grandeur. That was probably why my husband left me. He knew I would never leave him.

Knowing her husband better than he knew himself, Sara replied, "Leon's sleeping and needs time to process what has happened."

Pleased with her good luck, Sara listened attentively to the talking map.

"That hotel you mentioned is the world-renowned Fairmont Banff Springs Hotel, which was built by William Cornelius Van Horne in 1886 to promote tourism. The hotel was built in the classic European chateau style where the Bow and Spray Rivers converged. At the time, it was the world's largest hotel. In 1926 the hotel burned down. It was rebuilt. Heads of states and celebrities like George VI, Queen Elizabeth, Helen Keller, and Marilyn Monroe stayed there. Every guest was catered to. Can you imagine constructing a landing strip so that pilots could land their planes on the hotel grounds? Well, that happened. Oh, and not to forget the golfers. A first-class mountain golf course was also added to the grounds. It was luxury all the way."

What great input Sara thought, so much more interesting than trying to decode a finely typed brochure that she could hardly see. She couldn't wait to be surrounded by Bow Valley and all its grandeur. After a ten-minute bus ride, Sara and Maggie trudged upwards nearing the historical creation. The mountains as well as the crowds clutched them. Crowds and Sara didn't mix.

Cameras popped up like minute popcorn and you had to get out of the way regardless of where you were. Everyone wanted the perfect picture. Sara learned quickly to duck or to be randomly pushed.

Sara's eyes widened as the steeple chateau-like masterpiece commanded her undivided attention. It was all worth it, the nonsense at the airport, the untimely gondola ride down the mountain, the popping cameras, none of it mattered now. The most beautiful sight she had ever seen stared back at her with bursting pride. It must have known that Sara was an American and had been to Europe. Lacy white wedding-cake trim encased the tops of the towers and numerous windows, as the brown richness of the main hotel glistened.

"Intoxicating, I never knew Canada had such beauty," said Sara softly as I watched her. The awestruck look on Sara's face instantly reaffirmed for me why I was a tour director. The Americans, the Europeans, the Australians, the Asians, and other world travelers needed to experience our Canadian beauty. It was an awakening for many of them as they realized that our beauty might rival theirs, even surpass it.

Sara closed her mouth, not wanting to drool remembering long ago when she first saw a chalet against snow-covered mountains. Living in Connecticut, only an hour and a half from Vermont, Sara had skies on before she knew why skiing was her father's sanity, removing him from other's dependence, and a tedious company job that he hated. Every weekend, her father packed his four hyper kids into his unprepared station wagon and headed for Vermont. While the Metropolitan Opera blared, he waited for that moment—the hypnotic moment when the rambunctious four stopped fighting, fidgeting, and fell asleep. Then it was his time. Her mother refused to go. An empty house meant eight hours of stillness. Her mother never knew that her husband had discovered how to tranquilize us naturally.

Like mules on a trail, Maggie and Sara climbed until they reached the summit and stood looking down into Bow Valley.

"Sara, take a look. Do you see how the two rivers intersect? Over there are the hot springs, known for their rejuvenating power because of the sulfur water that is piped in."

Sara wished she could jump in the springs, at least knee-deep, but thought better of it. After all, she now represented the United States and wanted to make a good impression on the Canadian.

Sara hated the "Ugly American" syndrome and was determined to put her best foot forward but not in the hot springs. The hotel's front entrance awaited them. It looked innocent enough, but once inside a huge marble staircase halted them. "Sara, this particular staircase has a history all its own, a sad history. A young bride on her wedding day was descending down the gray-white polished marble steps with her groom beside her when a sudden gust of wind from an opened widow entangled her train. Down the stairs she fell. Her groom couldn't catch her. Death did." Sara cringed, such beauty, such despair. She carefully placed one foot in front of the other, one step at a time instead of pushing her legs like she usually did.

Maggie was sure in great shape, Sara thought, as she paused at the top of the stairs. Her stair-stepping workouts waned in comparison to whatever Maggie did. No matter what, she would keep up with Maggie. They reached their destination.

The walls were made of deep, dark cherrywood encrusted with inlaid marble. That rich woody scent permeated the air. You could smell the forest as it twisted and turned eventually leading to the ballroom. As if ready for battle, knights in armor lined the walls donning shiny metal face helmets while clutching drawn swords and shields. Silver goblets and artifacts waited as if expecting King Arthur and his medieval knights to arrive at any moment.

"Notice the coats of armor dotting the walls. They represent different families that reigned in power throughout the ages," I commented, not wanting Sara to miss a thing. But her head turned more than mine.

"A castle-like hotel in the middle of an alpine pine forest," Sara mused, peeping out of one of the encased windows. Catching a glimpse of William Cornelius Van Horne's statue, Sara saw him pointing towards the Bow Valley and realized why Van Horne was indignant that his masterpiece had been built backwards.

"How things have changed. Today a general manager wouldn't have cared about the hotel's position even if the guests had to crane their necks to appreciate the magnificent view."

Beyond the ballroom lay personalized shops sporting enticing wares that were carefully placed inside neatly draped windows. Sara's eyes were immediately transfixed with the porcelain figurines; the Yadros and Daltons beckoned her.

"Maggie, look at the detail, the proportions of the figurines. It's as if they might just respond to you as you appreciate their beauty." Sara wished people could be more like figurines, beautifully silent. Life would be so much easier.

I wasn't partial to figurines, nor did I care. Sara had a cultivated eye for beauty and I didn't.

Struggle didn't allow time for figurine fondness. Struggle allowed little time for any kind of appreciation. Struggle hounded me. I was usually in survival mode. Seeing the pure delight etched on Sara's face, I wished that I had some of it. Sara quickly noticed a hazy gaze from Maggie's usually spirited eyes. Sara's self-centeredness had masked her vision as it sometimes did.

One of Leon's mantras permeated her thoughts. *Do you think that it's all about you, what you think, and how you feel?*

Leon's coldness froze in her ears. Sara consciously redirected her energy considering what Maggie might like.

Next door, the colors of numerous indigenous paintings quickly grabbed my attention. Now, I was in my element. This shop contained Indian paintings and artifacts depicting graphic symbols from their struggling culture.

"Sara, those symbols on this totem pole represent hierarchy in the Indian culture, revealing their religious beliefs."

Sara grimaced knowing how much the ritualistic Indian culture numbed her mother. The totem poles didn't sacrifice. Sara studied the symbols.

"That's the plumaged head, Thunderbird, which was the chief of all guardian spirits and the protector of the Indian people. Being the most powerful of all the creatures, he was ruler and master of the skies. Actually the Indians believed that his wings created thunder and his flashing eyes created lightning.

"Underneath it is the prestigious Eagle, which symbolized great hunting skills and exceptional hearing and seeing. Any Indian's totem bearing the curved beak eagle was considered to be a visionary and the sacred down from the eagle's breast was a sign of peace and friendship used during welcoming ceremonies.

"That third symbol is the joyful messenger and healer, the hummingbird. With its long and very thin beak, the hummingbird was known for its healing powers during sorrowful and painful times."

"So these totem poles told stories about the different tribes?"

"Well, yes, but much more than that. They were actually visual biographies, neon lights that flashed friendship or warfare. Most Indians had a totem. It was part of their culture and religious beliefs."

Sara suddenly understood their unknowns and was thankful that she didn't need a totem to protect her. She only needed her powerful Lord. Grimacing, Sara knew she never would have made it as an Indian. They would have banished or sacrificed her.

Wanting Sara to enjoy all our cultural differences, I knew that high tea would soon be served on the patio and headed in that direction.

"Sara, we have a tradition here, high tea, which originally was brought over by the English, who were very formal, very elegant, and very proper." Being three-fourths English with ancestors dating back to the Mayflower, Sara knew formal. Having always been eligible for membership with the Daughters of the Revolution, Sara never applied, abhorring paper work and groups of unknown people. Like oil and water, she didn't mix, feeling vulnerable around too many people at one time. Even as a little girl, making friends and forcing words were torture. But elegant and proper was innately comfortable. She was drawn to it. Flashy television advertisements of high tea aboard cruise ships suddenly permeated her brain.

As the table neared, Sara wasn't disappointed. The beautifully matching porcelain teapots and perfectly arranged dainty teacups triggered her memory of another tea party, one from her childhood. The caterpillar from *Alice in Wonderland* puffed circular smoke rings right beside her. An overly stuffed four-tiered platter was quietly ushered in full of assorted scones dribbling blueberry, strawberry, and boysenberry glaze. Sara's instinct was to inhale one of each but quickly refrained reminding herself that no one was going to take it from her. Another one of Leon's reminders.

Observing Sara, I marveled at how the American chose a little bit of everything. *How did she keep her svelte figure?* I wondered. Sara seemed so carefree, so effortless, inhaling everything around her, the complete opposite of me.

"Maggie, what's the matter? Is it something that I said or didn't say? Did I take a scone that you wanted?" As Maggie's eyes brimmed with tears, Sara felt as though she had committed a Canadian grievance.

"He just left. He left me with my son and daughter and never came back."

"Who left you?"

"The pain, the unnerving pain is still there after all these years. It never goes away. It always waits for me. I can't get rid of it. There are no answers."

"Maggie, your husband, is that who left you?"

"He was so unhappy. I didn't know why. He refused to talk. He stopped working, wanting only hibernation, sleeping most of the day and night. The depression captured him. One morning the sofa was empty. His things were gone. He disappeared into thin air like the last homemade chocolate cookie on a well-visited tray. Panicking, I waited and waited. Each day, each month, each year passed without a single word from him. It was as though he had never been. The made-up explanations to my kids, the creeping uncertainty devoured me. I just don't..."

"Maggie, I'm so sorry. I mean who would do something so...but Maggie, your husband, sounds, depressed, unstable like mine. That depression, with all its ugliness also visited our sofa, devouring Leon. When he retired, Leon lost his powerful persona as a professor and nothing could replace it. No longer a leader and educator at the university, his purpose was skewed, and he questioned the title-less man he had become. Conversation stopped. Questions stopped. Feelings stopped. Leon drifted beyond my reach. The depression stole our relationship and Leon's soul. One day I had a compassionate husband and the next day an unwanted intruder had invaded our home. Physically, Leon never left me. But the man I married is nowhere to be found. Our dependent souls are no longer attached to one another, but are hanging ragged and torn beyond recognition. Chilling emptiness remains. Everyday I have trained myself to ignore the feeling pretending that it doesn't matter." Sara wanted so much to say something that connected her to Maggie's pain.

I was thankful for Sara's kind words. We were both vulnerable, somewhat broken, coping with a deep-veiled sadness that we couldn't change.

"Sara, I guess we both share uncertainty. Thank you for caring." As though on cue, a mournful bagpipe echoed its lamentations in the near distance. The stirring notes seemed to wrap themselves around me. Slowly, my unrequited sadness seeped away, and I couldn't wait to show Sara those legs in that classic Scottish kilt.

"Sara, another bit of European flair, yet this time from Scotland. This is a sight that you cannot miss, a Scottish piper complete with bagpipes, pleated kilt, and stockings." The intoxicating music led us around to the front of the hotel where perched high up on the stoop of a winding stairway stood the nicest pair of legs that Sara had seen in quite awhile. His skilled fingers moved up and down the gleaming black bagpipes while he artfully filled the sacks with just the right amount of air, caressing them with Scottish emotion.

"Maggie, he looks better in his skirt than I do," said Sara, thankful for the joyful musical serenade that was spirited and uplifting. You could see the Scottish highlands covered with Moorish fog.

Once again, my tour director persona was in charge, and I meant to keep it that way. My voiced personal feelings about my life were so unexpected, so unstoppable. I never shared with one of my tourists before and wasn't sure what the side effects might be. Little did I know how much it would alter relationships.

A DIAMOND IN THE ROUGH

The morning nagged me. It knew how important it was to start off on a positive note. Checking dispositions and body language, I was relieved to see satisfied, energized faces. It was amazing what a free day could do. Most of the guests were busy digesting bits of breakfast and exchanging mindless conversation with anyone who would listen.

Last evening was another matter. About twelve couples opted for the Canadian dinner with its unique entertainment. French characters reenacted episodes of our history. Before leaving for the outing, one outgoing Australian woman was concerned about Greta, a young German woman traveler who dined alone. Mrs. Kanga asked Greta to join them but she declined, which raised eyebrows and abrupt conversations. Adding insult to verbal injury, Greta thoroughly enjoyed herself only fueling the backlash.

What was it about a single woman on a trip who preferred her own company that sent shivers down other women's backs? Was her cherished independence a flashing neon sign?

I, too, have been guilty of flashing those neon signs. Traveling alone, my passion was not merely tasting primitive cultures but inhaling them. Usually this meant exploring far from the beaten bus tour trail opting for dirt paths with native sounds of shrieking monkeys, baying elephants, and cackling parrots. From a tour director's perspective, a bus full of inhalers would cause a lot of headache, so I was very glad that I had only one or two on my bus.

An unexpected note was quietly passed to me. It was from the honeymooners thanking me for the bottle of Banff champagne that waited for them in their makeshift honeymoon suite last night. Turning around, I locked onto two pairs of Israeli eyes that shared an unleashed joy causing a heart to race. My heart was unaccustomed to such a pace.

Then I saw Gerard. My heart skidded to a complete halt. Today I was determined that any possible mishaps would be handled by me without any assistance from him. Gerard seemed completely out of character, oddly relaxed, laughing, and joking with the patched-up patients, Dotty and Ariel sitting directly behind him. There were no ice packs or pillows nurturing Dotty's knees, so I assumed she was back in command of her rheumatoid arthritis.

Wafting bits of conversation huddled in the air like warmed coffee aroma.

"Gerard, thanks for your diversion yesterday on the mountain. I gave up and was sure that I was luncheon meat for two," commented Leon, liking Gerard the moment he intervened. There was a cold certainty about him. No hesitation, just action. Leon respected that and was drawn to its source like a magnet.

"I guess it was just a matter of being at the right place at the right time," replied Gerard, still stunned from the synthetic leg's response. It had unnerved him and brought 9/11 back––the anguish, the screaming, and the violence, like a perverse violator who refused to go away. It was the moment that shattered his regulated existence. The stench of jet fuel, the shattering of bulletproof glass, tangled bodies whose unstoppable squirting red blood covered him. His mangled best friend lay in his arms and stared the empty stare of death. He never shook it off and just diluted it anyway that he could.

"I guess you're glad that mountains aren't on the agenda today," paused Gerard studying the professor and noticing his wife's obsession for what flashed by the bus. Absorbed by the pure beauty, Sara didn't seem to want or need any feedback from her husband and there was none.

"Yes, Lake Louise sounds wonderfully flat," replied Leon. "Being from the southern tip of Texas, Canada's terrain has been a radical change for Sara and me. Where's your home?"

Part of his intrigue, Leon watched as Gerard inched down his red baseball cap a bit lower on his forehead, as his brown tinted sunglasses hovered underneath its brim.

"Washington, the Capitol," answered Gerard as the professor began to discuss metrics, statistics, and academia. Until recently, it defined who he was before forced to retire because of a weakened heart and perpetual panic attacks. Gerard detected the covered anguish lurking behind the professor's words. It mimicked his own. With only one leg, the professor achieved so much. Respect gushed out of Gerard as he reevaluated his own two legs.

"Maggie, have you done the extras yet?" Gus' whisper abruptly ended my nonchalant eavesdropping.

The numerous credit card voucher slips were sitting right next to me waiting, eager to be filled out by future thrill seekers, options included: Athabasca River rafting, a lake cruise with stops at Spirit Island, or enjoying canoeing on Lake McGillivray. Of course the trip wouldn't be complete without whale watching, or visiting Chinatown.

Oohs and Aahs sounded throughout the bus as I handed out the brochures for continued adventures. Credit cards flashed in and out of pockets like a relay race as specific boxes were checked on the payment vouchers.

Now the added adventures were very alluring. By the end of the day, one's energy could be totally gone. But once you paid for it, you went or made a donation. There were no refunds on cancellations. That was when my patience, wit, and counseling skills really kicked in. The event's sponsors prepared for a certain number of guests, organized, and paid their help accordingly. When numbers changed, the relationship with that specific enterprise was in jeopardy.

Counting the check marks, I breathed a sigh of relief. Leon and Dotty had not opted for additional activities. But Sara had checked everything and anything, even events that were scheduled for the same time. It had to be her teacher mania––nonstop energy. Watching Leon who could hardly move and Sara who never stopped, gave new meaning to the old adage that opposites attract.

My international visitors were from many countries. The New Zealanders and Aussies were a hardy bunch, lively and spirited. Exchanging bouts of laughter, a group of blonde-streaked, gray-haired ladies from New Zealand dominated the bus. Listening to them, you would think that they didn't have a care in the world. Looks were deceiving. All had just recently lost their husbands. After spending time with them last evening, I learned that this trip was actually a desperate fling, group therapy that they all needed. I wished that I could join their group since my husband might as well fall into that category.

The English couples were impeccably dressed, the English always looked as though they expected their beloved mother, the Queen. The men actually wore apparel that blended together, while the women fluttered in soft, fitted, spotless pastels. Glancing at my loose fitting, comfortable brown pants, I looked as though I were expecting a deer, which to an extent I was. Tomorrow, I would make more of a concentrated effort to visually impact my guests.

The German adrenaline level ran high as they bragged about river rafting and jumping out of helicopters. There wasn't an ounce of natural fat on any of them and the women held their own with a natural, confident style.

Make-up might not be a priority in Germany, but it certainly seemed to be in the Philippines. The Filipino women reminded me of beautiful, delicate figurines: perfect features, with perfect personalities, usually one delicate step behind their significant other. Right now, I was one delicate step behind Gus, which only irritated me. I was determined to get him back in his rightful position.

"Maggie, we're approaching the halfway point. It looks like roaming leg room might be needed especially for the Americans."

"We'll stop just up ahead where we usually do," I replied, making sure that my voice reeked of certainty. Hurrying off of the bus, Sara left Leon contentedly behind. It took Leon forever to get up, so Sara artfully climbed over him as carefully as possible much to the astonishment of others.

Sara was accustomed to doing things on her own, figuring things out. Right now, she left Leon's pain behind. Sara knew the pain. She fought it. She hated it. Every minute of everyday, it consumed Leon and their relationship.

"Sara, wait up," urged a voice. Sara reminded Dotty so much of her younger daughter, impulsive and headstrong.

"Dotty, how are your knees?" Sara answered reluctantly, trying to be as polite as possible since she was pulled away from her thoughts.

"Oh, my knees are used to the abuse, just not to this extent," answered Dotty, determined to connect with Sara on a deeper level. Those early foggy, California mornings probably nurtured her determined behavior. The routine, the dirt, and the constant crop care screamed survival. Dotty was tough and Sara empathized with her condition, but right now Sara didn't want to be around pain.

Don't be self-centered, her mother's words reverberated in her brain. Sara couldn't get away from her mother even if she wanted to which she didn't. Her mother's boulder-like stability never budged. It kept Sara grounded.

"Ariel really seems to enjoy Gerard and Leon," said Sara, hoping Dotty could see through the lifeless words. She didn't.

"Oh, Sara, you know when men are together, they bond as though they had never seen another man in their life. The chance to talk freely without being critiqued must be exhilarating. I haven't seen Ariel laugh this much in ages. Well, laughter doesn't come very readily on a back of a tractor, and to this day at ninety-one, he's still on one," replied Dotty, thankful that she was making headway with the teacher. She could use a bit of laughter herself and thought Sara might just be the answer.

"Ariel is still raising crops?" questioned Sara, somewhat startled and started to pay a bit more attention to the farmer's wife.

"Well, not exactly, when Ariel retired and sold the farm, he just couldn't adapt to having both feet on the ground, so the town hired him to be the town hall's grounds caretaker. He's still out there by six o'clock in the morning. Regardless, some things never change."

Sara peered behind Dotty's words and was drawn to the persistent lady.

We didn't get delayed on the roaming stops. They were only to stretch, breathe in some uncirculated air, and air out any unwanted conversation. Gus never got out. I always did. It redirected me, helping me showcase my country with all its unique history.

Lake Louise was coming up right around the bend, so I nurtured the intrigue. "How would you like to be renamed three times? It happened to Lake Louise. The lake was first named by the natives who called it the Lake of Little Fishes. In 1882, a worker for the Canadian Pacific Railway renamed the lake Emerald Lake because of its emerald color. In 1884, Emerald Lake was changed once again to Lake Louise honoring Princess Louise Caroline who was the fourth daughter of Queen Victoria and married to the governor-general of Canada.

"Lake Louise was one of the first mountaineering centers, and the Canadian Pacific Railway imported Swiss guides to develop an extensive trail system that extended into the back country." The grabber worked. I had every ear and eye focused on me, attentively. That was just the way I liked it, no competition.

"In 1890, a simple log cabin served as a day lodge. But in 1893, fire consumed the structure. But it was destroyed over and over again. In 1982, a seemingly fire-resistant chateau survived with enlarged meeting rooms, restaurants, and lodging facilities. Chateau Lake Louise became a renowned entertainment center with cliental from all over the world. Next to the chateau, the Rocky Mountains offered skiers the thrill of their lives with helicopter skiing and still do.

"Inside, the Mount Temple Wing was built as a tribute to the tallest peak in Banff National Park and has an interior cathedral-like ceiling. In the ballroom, you'll see massive murals depicting scenes of the surrounding wilderness. Heritage Hall has five huge handmade stained glass windows that highlight the wildlife creatures: eagles, bears, mountain goats, and wolves. Sixty-five million dollars transformed a diamond in the rough into a dazzling emerald. Make sure you leave some time to see it. Feet shuffled.

"Check your watches, please. It's now one o'clock and you need to be back on the bus in two hours, by three o'clock, or the bus will leave without you." Hearing it in my dreams, it was my classic line. Now whether or not I would really have the heart to leave someone behind remained to be seen.

The bus unloaded by designated rows and always reminded me of departing from a strict elderly teacher's elementary classroom, except hands were not clasped behind backs and mouths were not closed. Good thing, buses were hard enough on tourists and mine looked eager to depart, all except Leon.

Leon hated drawing attention to himself. Disembarking from this bus could have been a hit feature from the movie, *The Man Everyone Waited For.* He didn't want to hear the pitiful comments. It enraged him. So he waited until everyone had gotten off including Sara who compounded his handicapped plight. Buses were not made for the handicapped. Thinking back, he recalled seeing no accommodations in the brochure for those with special needs. It was presumed that anyone planning a trip touring the Canadian Rockies needed to have two functioning legs that worked in unison, effortlessly. That was logical and he kicked himself with his one good leg realizing how foolish it was for him to think that he could keep up with Sara or anyone else for that matter. But he hadn't counted on the close encounter with the bear. It tore at him mentally as well as physically. Gus had somehow sensed his despair and latched on to him like a submarine's sonar maneuvering him slowly down the aisle while his obstinate leg objected.

"Leon, once we're off the bus, there's a rest area close by with numerous benches where you can relax and enjoy the scenery."

Enjoy the scenery, thought Leon, why that was the last thing on his mind. How could anyone expect him to enjoy anything when he was in such pain? No one knew how much he hurt. He refused to vocalize it. Maybe with just a little extra personal attention he could make it. Gus cared and that wasn't part of his job description. Leon was intrigued. Why would anyone want to put up with temperamental individuals week after week? And to be ordered around by a woman was unimaginable. Apparently, it didn't rattle Gus, and Leon wanted to know why.

Gus had a schoolboy grin on his face as he presented Leon with a sugary chocolate-covered, sprinkled doughnut. He undoubtedly procured it from an obscure takeout that catered only to emerald-uniformed policeman and worn-out bus drivers. Sweets attracted Leon like statistics. He could never get enough of them. His slightly padded waist could attest to it.

"Gus, how do you do it? Meeting all the wants of all these people?"

"Well, that's why I enjoy it. The fact that I'm needed...by the tourists and others...well, especially Maggie, who I'm sure would deny any hint of it. The very thought would probably send her into a tailspin, like a rudderless boat. Once in a while though when Maggie flashes me one of her approving looks, it works like adhesive and straps me in that seat for another hundred miles. The routine of a stationary job or a relationship for that matter would devour me. Routine and consistency is not genetically part of my makeup. That's why I probably have never married, or even come close to a meaningful relationship. Any feelings that I may have for Maggie are purely lopsided. Men are invisible to her, especially bus drivers." Leon listened attentively.

"You know, Leon, it's really not my place, but Sara really needs to stay with the group instead of going off by herself. Things can happen out here."

"Do me a favor and tell her. She won't listen to me."

Sara was glad to be off of the bus. There was just something about open spaces that she craved. Being cramped in a bus seat with her long giraffe-like legs and roaming neck was unpleasant enough, but knowing that Leon expected her to wait and stay with him was just ridiculous. She couldn't.

The "Emerald" was just waiting to be explored. Bounding up the mountainous path, Sara was startled as she almost stumbled on top of one of the male tourists in a compromising position. He was making a deposit. Waiting one minute longer was not an option. Quickly redirecting her astonishment, Sara turned quickly, too quickly and almost toppled down the steep path. Regaining her balance, she fixated on the teal-green-colored lake. Calming, it refocused her.

What was it about water? Sara paused. In any form, it transported her, clarifying annoying thoughts. The green lake reminded Sara of the green-blue ocean water about an hour from her house. Sara loved the ocean, but rarely got a chance to spend time there.

Sara was back on their first date on the beach with Leon. It all seemed so right. But it was all so wrong. Actually Leon hated the beach and the sun and anything that was outdoors. Through no fault of his own but that it reminded him of his twelfth summer when his mother assigned all his brothers and sisters the daily backbreaking task of picking cotton from sunup to sundown. Leon tried to please Sara but her heart belonged to the outdoors. Sara never really knew his heart didn't until it was too late.

One thing Leon never tried to camouflage was his ability to move, to get around. From the very beginning, he had reminded Sara that she had two good legs that worked effortlessly and should find someone with the same equipment. Sara never listened, never cared, never considered. Maybe if she had...

Sara thought Leon needed a positive, limitless life force by his side. That isn't at all what he needed or wanted. Leon was limited. It was Sara who finally realized it. Once she did, a part of her vanished knowing that her passions would never be shared. Sometimes, it was just too hard to admit that she was now more lonely with him than without him.

As she clamored towards the historic chalet, the snow-swept winds of Lake Tahoe howled in her thoughts. Skiing with her father in Lake Tahoe's mountains challenged both of them and almost did away with them. Sara inadvertently led her dad down one of the most treacherous ski slopes as its black-flag waved them on. Before their goggles had defogged, she comprehended her negligent error, straight vertical screamed at them. This was not heli-skiing, but you would never have known it. Trying to maintain an upright, vertical position was impossible, so they both sat down and slid until the bottom of the mountain awkwardly greeted them. Needless to say, their posterior ends got more attention than they deserved. But the terror cemented them together because Sara's dad understood her, her impulsive nature and accepted it. More often than not, she just didn't think things through.

Leon didn't understand her impulsiveness. As each day ended, Sara realized that she didn't marry someone like her father. Leon didn't know her and didn't want to know her. At first, Leon's differences absorbed her, now they only separated.

Then she heard it, approaching steps getting nearer and nearer.

"That's the one over there. Let's get her. Sara knew only too well what this was about. It was that man that she saw quite by accident. Men don't like to be embarrassed by anyone especially a woman. Near the chalet, Sara ran in blending with the others.

Being in danger was foreign to her. Her job as a teacher demanded that she put others first and she did. Taking care of herself never really entered her mind. Leon was ten minutes away, but it could have been a million miles. Sara didn't want to end up in the lake so she needed to think it through. The bus wasn't too faraway. It was just a matter of timing. She needed a diversion. The fire alarm would have to do. Everything prevented her from pulling the handle. It was wrong. She knew it. At school, she punished others for pulling alarms. But it wasn't school and she wasn't a kid. She counted, pulled the alarm, and ran like everybody else.

Making it back to the bus, Sara was red-faced, totally out of breath, but breathed more easily once she did. Very content, Leon munched on doughnuts. Sara was in red alert and her fear almost burst. Forcing calmness, Sara stopped. Leon would hunt the man down and destroy him. Here and now, their trip would end. Sara silenced the words. The man wasn't on their bus. Sara devoured one of Leon's doughnuts.

Because of the clock's hands, Maggie relaxed. Unlike the gondola thriller, everyone was headed back. Faces and body language told it all. As a tour director, you listened to what was said, but more importantly what wasn't. Listening, satisfaction oozed.

For a memorable trip, well-being and camaraderie needed to find one another. Without any assistance from me, they did. Like high school, little cliques formed. The more talkative, well-dressed, slower moving tourists gravitated towards one another; while the more athletic sneaker-clad group dared each other on. The editors, the notetakers, sat together, and didn't miss any of it.

We even had our very own cheerleading squad. On their benches, a group of contented women gabbed gleefully enjoying other's fun.

A big hurrah swept through the air when everyone returned on time. Flashing Gus one of my approving looks, I was quite pleased. We were ahead of schedule and headed for the Columbia Icefield.

HOT CHOCOLATE WITH
THE PROFESSOR

A long-distance athlete in training, the bus climbed, as it slowly inched its way up the mountainous terrain. My words didn't hesitate. They knew this land, loved it, and didn't need any prompting.

"At two o'clock," I stopped, as puzzled faces squinted out the window. Some were unfamiliar with the lingo, so I pointed out the clock positions, feeling like an airline stewardess. "You can see an endangered woodland caribou that ought to feel very comfortable since it's protected in Jasper National Park. Notice its large antlers and large hoofs. The male and female are indistinguishable."

"That one is gorging himself. He must be a male," Sara commented assuredly to Leon who was engaged at two o'clock.

"We'll be going through the park, and, if you look closely, you'll be able to see more wildlife as we continue our elevation."

"Look over there at nine o'clock. It's Rudolph." Laughed Leon, pleased that he had seen it before anyone else. Maybe they would appreciate his alertness if not his mobility.

"Yes, Rudolph is the largest member of the deer family and can grow up to seven feet tall and weigh up to 1,500 pounds. With his massive antlers and size, he definitely looks like a sled-pulling reindeer but is in fact a male moose."

Leon was determined to go beyond his pain and enjoy himself if only for a moment or two. When he sat, his leg retreated and relaxed. His mind needed to follow suit.

"What were those little moving white cotton-ball specs towards the top of the mountain at twelve o'clock?" piped Leon, wishing that he had just a little of their agility.

"Good eye, Leon. Those are white mountain goats that usually roam in groups of fifty to sixty, preferring narrow rocky ledges. Up close, they are rather comical with beards and short black horns."

Sara burst out loud. "You know the fairy tale, the bearded *Billy Goats Gruff*?" Grabbing her binoculars, she wanted a close-up of that bearded fairy-tale creature.

Martha, probably the head cheerleader from Australia, piped up, "Our fairy tales are of a slightly different nature. The characters are also bearded, but human, and very real.

"The Aborigines, the original inhabitants of our country, have been well-documented throughout our history. Their immigrations can be traced back 70,000 years ago during the last Ice Age when they crossed a land bridge, which connected Indonesia to Australia and Tasmania. Twenty thousand years later, immigration colonized all of Australia."

My ears perked up; something other than kangaroos, wonderful.

"There were about five hundred different tribes who had their own territory and dialect. A common language didn't exist. If they had shoes, they would have easily worn them out since all they did was walk, never staying in one place very long. Nature was their spiritual power and altering their habitat was prohibited. They believed that creation ancestors were both animal and humans who left their spirits in the mountains and rocks. Each clan had sacred sites where their spirits lived after they died.

"Each tribe had a totem, rather like the American Indians, and that totem determined both personal and tribal relationships. When a boy came of age, his body was painted with earth tones as deep slashes were carved into his back and appendages. If he survived the brutality, his healing scars represented manhood and respect within the tribe.

"The Aborigines used very primitive boomerangs and spears to hunt game. Forget the silver. When they consumed edible roots, stone tools and carved wooden bowls were used. But their primitive existence was altered.

"In 1788, the British needed a new penal colony for its prisoners and decided that Sydney, Australia, would be perfect since it was desolate and inhabited only by the Aborigines who had no system of government, no homes, and no laws. The British established terra nullius, which meant the land belonged to no one and took the land away from the Aborigines.

The Aborigines fought back but without any luck. The Aborigines became a sport; they were the hunted. Reservations and church missions became their homes."

For once in her life, Sara actually listened and learned something historical. Martha had to be a retired teacher and Sara felt an immediate connection with her.

Martha continued, "In the early 1900s, the British wanted to segregate the Aborigines. They were told where to live and whom to marry. Granted citizenship in 1967, the Aborigines became educated and in 1972 achieved independence.

"Today many prefer the outback, living in the desert. Their backward ways and appearances attract the curious but also fuel discrimination."

Sara never considered that each country had its own distinct discrimination problems.

"My turn," Maggie interrupted. "Get ready for some glaciers, ice, and snow. Columbia Icefield has the largest accumulation of snow south of the Arctic Circle. The Athabasca Glacier is over four hundred years old and one thousand feet thick. An elongated Ford Explorer especially fitted with raft-like tires will assist you up the ice field allowing you to experience the glacier firsthand. You may even want to take a sip of the frigid water, which is numbing but exhilarating."

Glancing at the glacier, Sara was disappointed while excitement surged around her. She had skied higher mountains than this many times in many places.

As Maggie watched the Martin-like Explorer steadily ascend up the glacier packed full with her anxious tourists, a saddened pair of brown eyes gazed momentarily into hers.

"I'm just not agile enough for any of this," commented Leon as Maggie helped steady him as well as his hot chocolate.

"Leon, not everyone is meant to climb glaciers. You're probably doing more than anyone ever expected."

Leon felt his barriers collapse as a long sigh tumbled out of his mouth. He felt so inadequate. I was drawn to this professor more than I wanted to be. Leon needed what Sara couldn't possibly give him: attention. She was too young and much too self absorbed. Maybe I could seal the cracks.

"My husband also had some health issues." I felt myself opening up aware that I also had cracks that needed sealing.

"Maggie, I don't know if Sara confided in you, but there was a time when I didn't even think that I'd be able to get off our couch."

"Leon, I know how Sara must've felt because my husband, well, ex-husband was attached to his couch as well."

"Those Italian leather couches. They just make them too comfortable," replied Leon, watching my face then realizing that the conversation had turned, it was now about me. Before I knew it, shadowy thoughts revealed themselves. The pain oozed out of me like rainwater on a desert cactus.

I continued, "It was all so unexpected. One minute I had a life and the next it was taken from me. I didn't ask for it to happen and no one asked me. He left without a word, taking my dignity and self-respect. Everyday, it still haunts me." Leon turned away as an awkward silence filled the air. The violation he felt when his first wife left him rushed through his entire body.

"I apologize. I didn't mean to make you feel uncomfortable. It's just that you remind me of him."

Regardless of any potential pain, Leon wished with all his might that he were nuzzled next to Sara on that oversized mountain-climbing Explorer. Being a professor at a university, women occasionally confided in him, but certainly not on a bus tour with his wife a mere glacier away.

The professor's uneasiness unglued me. The cardinal rule of any tour director was broken. Personal involvement with clients was prohibited. This conversation needed to be adjusted quickly, carefully.

"The mind is just so unpredictable. One minute, a person copes with life and the next minute clings to desperation." As if rehearsed, Leon lit up like a freshly adorned Christmas tree. Mental illness was his passion.

"There's just so much that we don't know about the mind. So many variables are involved. After my open-heart surgery, I just couldn't adjust to my weakened condition, being ripped out of one body and jammed into another. My anger suffocated me. I cordoned myself off from anyone and everyone. Mental illness steals without permission. It's difficult for significant others to witness the withdrawal. Sara tried her best to conceal her emptiness, but it flashed like Morse code. Healing comes with time, if it comes at all. Those who survive fight for glimpses of sanity."

Maggie replied, "But it's that rejection that hurts so much. I still don't know what drove him away. There are too many gaping holes. Often in the morning, I'm focused and directed. Suddenly I can't seem to navigate throughout the remainder of the day."

"Maggie, some things cannot be clarified because sometimes there are just no answers." My cooling hot chocolate lost its flavor as my mind switched gears. Neutral was not a comfortable place for me. Words abandoned me. My thoughts were averted to the glacier expedition.

Sara left Leon in very capable hands. Maggie's expression convinced her. Without a second thought, she headed for the Explorer, curious to see what waited at the top of the mountain. All seats were spoken for like the morning bus rides to school when she was in seventh grade. Before she knew it, she positioned herself beside Gerard the secretive man who had witnessed her husband's hairy bear encounter.

Slowly, Gerard's blue baseball cap inched its way back from his face. Beside him sat the binocular addict––the teacher who had intrigued him from the very beginning. Sara felt completely at ease while she conversed with this man of few words. This was unusual since she usually had no interest in strangers. Maybe it was the cap. It reminded her of the one that inched its way over her face when she pedaled furiously on her bike as long as her legs permitted. Whatever it was, Sara talked more freely and openly with Gerard than she had expected. His easy manner and ready smile were intoxicating. She was unarmed.

"You seemed shocked when my husband's leg was ripped apart and didn't bleed. It must have seemed awfully strange when the smell of plastic permeated the air. Some of his good friends don't even know that he has a bloodless leg. It's all part of the professor guise, the mystique behind the title."

"Yes, titles can be deceiving. I work for the Department of Defense, but in the accounting department. Instead of devising strategic battle plans, I focus on numbers and their amounts." Sara's eyes lit up.

"So you're the one who orders gold-plated bathroom accessories when they need to be replaced."

"You must be referring to the recent, scandalized story regarding the military base that has dominated much of the media. It was tasteless, but accurate."

"How can you not know where your money goes? I mean how can the Defense's accounting department not know how their money is being allocated? At my school, every penny has to be accounted for, supplies are assigned and distributed, even paper clips. If something needs to be replaced, it usually takes forever but the price doesn't change. That's just a school, a mere microcosm of society. But your department is supposed to know exactly what's happening and where it's happening. Isn't it?"

"Of course, you have a valid point. It's an awkward situation to say the least. We're doing our best to ensure that it doesn't happen again. May I call you Sara?" Sara craved politeness. Somehow Gerard sensed it.

"Have you spotted a bald eagle yet with those extra magnified eyes of yours? Just after we left Jasper National Park, I spotted one." Quietly Gerard pulled out his own concealed pair of travel binoculars. A sudden jolting of the Explorer interrupted them.

Within seconds, a comical voice of sorts filled the air. It was Dave, the glacier guide who informed them what and what not to expect once they reached the top of the ice mound. Out of his mouth tumbled one off-color joke after another. Annoyed, Sara wasn't at all impressed.

"Why doesn't Dave audition for a comedy act instead of toting a group of bus-lagged tourists up a historical glacier? Certainly there's nothing funny about that."

"Sara, where's your sense of humor? This is a seasonal job that lasts three months if that. I bet that his other nine are spent as a nurse. Nurses often have a very odd sense of humor, even tasteless at times. But do you blame them? Look at all they have to deal with: bed pans, late hours, last-minute schedule changes, irritable patients, and often incurable diseases. Probably, it's his therapy as well as paid, quirky entertainment which is all part of his job. Once we return to the lodge, a tip will more than likely be expected and appreciated."

Needy nurse or not, Sara wasn't amused. A teacher was examined every minute of every day. Every word that came out of her professional mouth was listened to and often repeated: whether defining a noun or verb or giving instructions on how to write an essay, sentences had to be accurate and correct. Conversations with concerned parents had to be mentally edited and carefully executed or one's teaching career could be quickly extinguished by one stroke of an administrator's pen. Sara felt her flushed cheeks.

"I just don't think that this is the time or place for a comedian."

"Sara, what could possibly be a better time or better place? After all we're on vacation, which means fun, some needed relaxation, a bit of entertainment, and most of all, the ability to let your mind unwrap, doesn't it? Maybe you could put your bias in a traveling case for a while and try to enjoy the frustrated nurse. It wouldn't hurt, would it?"

Sara knew what Gerard was trying to say. She didn't know what *fun* was. How could she? There was never enough time or energy. Now she had an opportunity to experience it.

A few seats ahead of her, Sara couldn't help, but notice that Dotty and Ariel were certainly enjoying the glacier climb. You never would have known that only a few days ago Dotty's knees were submerged in frigid ice water, unable to bend. They were bending now. Dotty had the biggest grin on her face as she prompted the irritating nurse with her own sense of humor. Dave wasn't at all impressed. It was his show and he wanted it to keep it that way. Dotty persisted. Others jumped in. It was all for one and one for all. It wasn't Dave's show anymore.

Sara couldn't help but relax, enjoying the spontaneity. Humor needed an opportunity to reveal itself and Sara hadn't seen it in an awfully long time. Sharing a life with someone who experienced constant pain left little time for idle laughter. But there wasn't any pain here. Instead, bus-lagged nerves uncovered an abundant source of energy that was just waiting to burst. Overinflated balloons soared except Dave's, which collapsed on the ground deflated and defeated. His rancid remarks abruptly ceased. His face tightened. He looked as though he couldn't wait to get this persistent group off his vehicle.

"Isn't it great how an unruly mob can derail someone?" Sara chuckled as the corners of her mouth relaxed.

Abruptly Gerard was pulled in by her deliberate choice of words. His own balloon suddenly sank and was covered by a mist of black smoke, a panic attack. A horrible stench clogged his nostrils. He choked. He blocked it. He didn't want to burden Sara with his own derailing. He forced himself to concentrate on the calming coolness, which etched itself on the window.

Sara noticed everything and was often told that she was much too observant, much too intense. She never listened. Now was no exception. In an instant, Gerard's face clouded over like a winter's day losing its joyful light. Sara's instinct wanted to pry, but her common sense held her back. She recognized pain. Pain couldn't be hurried, revealing itself only when it was good and ready.

"I was a bit taken back by your choice of words, 'How an unruly mob can derail someone,' since I have experienced it myself. It was on 9/11, that infamous day when——"

Simultaneously, the unnerving events also unfolded in Sara's mind as she recalled that infamous day. "Sara, Sara, turn on your television." It was like a warrior's cry as the art teacher across the hall pounded relentlessly on her door interrupting her half-taught language lesson. Just as she adjusted the monitor, an unwieldy plane plummeted sideways into one of the Twin Towers in New York City. As flames leaped indiscriminately burning anything and everything in its way, frantic people clung desperately to the mangled sides of the violated building. Within seconds, another plane followed close behind slicing into the remaining tower. Fireballs rained down on paralyzed victims as horror controlled their legs and arms. Flaming debris limited choices. For most of the trapped victims, jumping was the only option. Much to the horror of many, one by one, individuals chose death instead of roasting in the deadly bonfire.

Sara blocked her mind as her students' drawn petrified faces looked to her for comfort and answers. Then without notice, the newscaster blurted out that terrorists violated the airspace with three planes stuffed with explosives. The third plane was headed for the Department of Defense.

Sara's mind suddenly unjammed. She knew the man sitting beside her didn't view the terrorist attack from the safety of a television monitor. How much did he see? How much did he anguish? Were his eyes saturated with deadly black rainfall? Were his ears filled with agonizing cries that only wanted mercy? Sara knew true terror by experiencing it. You had to be there. Terror wasn't comforted by well-meaning platitudes. It didn't work that way. Embarrassed, Sara wished that she hadn't made such a fuss about the irritating nurse. None of it mattered now. The black rainfall hung heavy in the air. The silence was broken as Gerard's thoughts penetrated Sara's. Should he chance it? Would she fall apart?

"Sara, I was there. The plane that rammed into the Department of Defense detonated itself right next to my office." Sara's face showed no uneasiness.

"My closest buddy worked in that office. Once the plane hit, all that I felt was a huge vibrating thud then a tremendous scorching heat that burst from the plane's heart. The immortal screams still haven't stopped."

For once in her life, Sara didn't know what to say. She wondered how much the plane had stolen from Gerard.

"My buddy's name was listed among the missing. I knew he wasn't missing but my own shock silenced me. He died in my arms cradled in his own blood-soaked oxford shirt. Before he died, his eyes asked why? I couldn't answer him then and I can't answer him now. Sometimes there are no reasons, no answers."

For a fleeting moment, Sara wished she had chosen any other seat, anywhere on that van. But just for a moment. Then her instinct took over.

"I, too, have lost someone very close to me and didn't have any answers. That night I promised my grandmother that I would visit her but never did. Instead, I went out to dinner with a friend. That selfishness cost me dearly. Later that selfish night, I woke up, startled, feeling a deadly chill rip through my entire body. My grandmother's face locked onto mine and wouldn't let me go. Choking, my tears suffocated me. I knew she was gone and the morning confirmed it. I never even had the chance to tell her why I broke my promise. Now, only death knew."

A comforting closeness seeped into Gerard. It didn't need to be questioned or answered. It no longer consumed him.

Abruptly, the Explorer's doughnut-sized tires halted. Dave's non-authoritative voice announced that they had reached their icy destination, the glacier's top. None too soon, one by one, the cramped occupants carefully lowered themselves with the assistance of a retractable ladder to the ice field below. Sara had no idea how high off the ground they were and almost slipped when her right foot misjudged the last rung. Instinctively, Gerard's hand reached out, steadied her, preventing a head-on collision with a waiting snow mound.

Dotty and Ariel were lowered and orchestrated the ladder's rungs without any mishaps. Embarrassed, Sara knew that if Dotty's arthritic knees could handle this workout, surely hers could, too. She hoped that they hadn't noticed. They did.

"Sara, so your young, agile knees had trouble navigating that ladder?" commented Ariel grinning a farmer's grin as he plodded through the frozen snow.

Time unraveled. His footsteps echoed those of the ancients as the ancient layers of ice held him up. With Dotty hanging on his right arm, he motioned to Sara and Gerard. Sara couldn't believe that she was not as sure-footed as the others. After all, she had spent her entire childhood up in Connecticut fastened to a pair of skates or skis.

With her father never far from her side, her young legs wobbled on a pond's slippery ice as her skates tried to hold her up like an unsteady colt. With daily practice and unwavering support, her legs eventually learned how to straighten themselves. She once again felt her father by her side and her legs quickly adjusted to the icy terrain.

"Sara, I'm right behind you," quipped Gerard. She wished he wasn't. All she needed now was to fall backwards into his instinctive arms. Ahead of her, freshly made, deepening footprints urged her on. Like arrows from a bow, numerous arms and legs were all headed in one direction towards the renowned, melting glacier water with its rejuvenating powers. Irritating Dave mentioned that long ago tribal Indians believed that the coldness of the water numbed harmful spirits and brought calmness to infirmities.

Sara couldn't wait to get a mouthful of that spiritual water. Before she left the comforts of the Explorer, she tucked an empty-covered coffee cup into her unwilling parka. Maybe the numbing spirits would help Leon with his grueling leg pain and allow him to enjoy at least some of this trip. Sara felt guilty leaving him in the lodge.

A year ago, her parents had carefully planned every possible detail of this prepaid anniversary extravaganza. Sara was determined to enjoy every bit of it. Even up until the very last minute though, the idea of actually going to Canada seemed unrealistic. Only after the planes' roaring engines confirmed a safe takeoff did Sara really know that Canada was more than just a thought.

Ahead of her, Ariel and Dotty reached the crowded watering hole and dipped their makeshift containers into the chilly slush.

"Sara, over here where there's more elbow room." Hastened Dotty knowing full well that Sara was probably feeling ill at ease without her professor by her side. As Sara bent slowly down towards the water, the deceiving ice suddenly gave way. She tumbled indiscriminately into its numbness.

Whirling backwards, her mind heard the frantic cries of Eric, her younger brother as he fell boot first into an icy fishing hole. His stubborn arctic boot caught itself on an ice-caked rake and wouldn't let go. It was Sara's rake that pulled him into the freezing water and Sara's rake that pulled him out.

Helping arms tugged at her as the spiritual water surged uninvited into her mouth. Fear wasn't a possibility; it was too cold. All she could think of was gulping down a steaming cup of hot chocolate loaded with whipped cream and nutmeg. Sara hung on to that thought like a crisp, dry-cleaned coat on its hanger. Her chances of getting out of this spiritual waterhole dimmed like a cold winter's sunset. Would Leon know? Leon knew everything. Her right leg was numb. Her left leg wasn't far behind. Then from out of nowhere, Dave's commanding arms somehow grabbed on to her willing parka and yanked her onto the bank of the slippery ice. Like they were on a mission, blankets wrapped themselves around her. Sara was a giant papoose being slowly urged along by a line of obedient warriors headed up by their fearless leader, Dave.

Circulation cautiously returned to her twitching limbs as Sara was tucked every which way into a front seat. Eyes fastened on to her like buttons on a shirt.

Self-conscious, Sara's mind flooded with unwelcomed memories of runways, onlookers, and flashing cameras. It only took one step on that runway to convince Sara that modeling was not part of her genetic makeup. The more they starred, the more she winced, wanting only to strut off that walkway and never strut back. Sara disliked attention and now was no exception.

Jammed eyes needed to be diverted. Gerard stuffed bills into the empty tip jar. Contagious, soon, bills of all amounts overflowed. Without hesitation, Dave expertly reshuffled the bills into an old hat that hung innocently next to the microphone attachment. Grateful, Dave's eyes glistened while others softened, giving way to acceptance. Sometimes an unscheduled event changed everything.

The lodge was in sight. As the blankets' warmth saturated her, Sara vowed never to trust ice again, without a glass.

Leon was right in the middle of his own unscheduled event. He fell, spilling hot chocolate everywhere, etching an unwanted trail towards his seat. Leon hated being the center of attention more than Sara.

Horrified, Sara's thawed arms and legs approached the tangled figure before her.

"Sara, what in the world of glaciers happened to you?" Leon's wit oozed out as he gazed at his saturated wife.

"Leon, it was an accident, really nothing."

Selfishly, Sara had relished the time away from Leon. It had unwrapped her sense of obligation, not worrying, not watching, not waiting for the fall, not waiting for the pain, not waiting for the cursing, and not waiting for the unwelcomed visitor that reminded Sara that she had two good legs instead of one.

Maggie didn't know who to be more concerned, about the downed professor or his watered-down wife. What was about this Texan couple? She heard things were bigger and better in Texas. But did it follow them wherever they went, even the mishaps?

A few moments earlier, I thoroughly enjoyed my conversation with the professor, probably too much. Then like a radar detector, his wife appeared out of nowhere. Staring in disbelief, I didn't know who to help first. Like a well-practiced drill, Sara urged her husband up supporting him while the determined floor resisted her. Others reached out as the embarrassed professor became untangled and landed in his seat. Suddenly my mouth remembered how to sympathize.

"Sara, let me help you. What happened? Didn't you stay with the others?" Sara wasn't listening. Trying to calm her husband, Sara was locked in her own world. By the professor's profanity, I was certain that Leon had some type of naval background, if not a naval career. Sara tried to soften the verbal outbursts, but couldn't knowing that Leon secretly wanted her to share the embarrassment because she left him.

"The ice, it just gave way near the spiritual watering hole. One minute, Ariel and Dotty were beside me, and the next thing I knew, I was looking out instead of looking in. Dave grabbed me and pulled me out as I turned into a fine, chilled glass of Marlowe wine."

Of all the guides to get on the tour, Dave, the frustrated nurse. It was difficult to believe that he was even with the group on the ice as he was habitually known to stay in the Explorer, working on the return part of his stage show. I shuddered at the comments that Sara and her husband would make on their valued evaluation forms. I may not even have a job by the end of this trip. The professor wasn't happy. He demanded to meet this Dave. Luckily Dave was nowhere to be found, which was not a surprise. There was only one lodge in town for tour guides and tourists. There would be no place to conveniently disappear once everyone had settled in for the night.

Right now, I needed an upgrade, a prepaid dinner for two and a larger room, a suite where the professor would have more room and not be assaulted with slippery floors. Other guests might complain about their limited accommodations once they heard about the suite, but I would take my chances. A lifeline for any tour director was upgrading. Whatever it took, I had to subdue the professor's anger.

LODGE IN THE MOUNTAINS

Gerard couldn't wait to get his feet in that canoe. Living in Washington, DC, left little time for relaxed feet. He wondered if others craved the natural pace, the softness of the outdoors, untouched by man's interfering fingerprints. After that tumble with the spiritual water hole, Gerard wondered if Sara's itinerary would include the lake cruise. He secretly wished that he was the one who pulled Sara out of the water hole. The professor's angry words still lingered in his mind and embarrassed him. They didn't affect Sara at all. Maybe Sara didn't hear them. If Sara were his, but she wasn't.

It didn't bother Dotty one bit that her husband was too tired to view the lake's reflected sunset. She was delighted to see Gerard and get that chance to really talk to him alone.

"Gerard, maybe we can keep this canoe upright?" prompted Dotty.

"Are any others coming?"

Dotty jabbered to the guide. *What was it about women*, thought Gerard. They could have multi-conversations simultaneously and know exactly what was going on in each one. Gerard wished that he had that ability.

Gerard was a powered lens that zoomed in on the details. If he didn't, he wouldn't have his job and certainly wouldn't have Gwena. He wondered if it were his job that kept her at his side. He was so sure that they were going together on this trip that he made reservations for both of them. Then the rejection, Gwena just declined. She couldn't or wouldn't take the time off. Surely, her practice could wait. Her clients could do without her for a week. But he couldn't and was devastated. He didn't want to care this much but he did.

Dotty sensed something different about Gerard. This certainly wasn't the casual Gerard that was so entertaining on the bus. Dotty picked up on his quietness like a Geiger counter. Gerard felt Dotty's sincerity. Right now he didn't want to be unearthed and engaging, but it was useless. He was no match for the farmer's wife with knobby knees and four o'clock mornings etched on her face.

"Gerard, just look at the blending colors how they sink so easily as if directed. You know, it's the complete opposite of the sunrise when the colors can't wait to come out one by one." The Geiger counter started ticking.

"You may be right. The water does seem to pull the colors down. Usually my sunrises and sunsets are masked with tinted dark windows since I'm cordoned off in my office. It's an exception when I really get to see the colors in their true light without the artificial decoy."

"Now that's an interesting word." Dotty's face was just too interested.

Gerard gave Dotty one of his artful accountant grins. The grin latched on to her and pulled her back. She was forty again with tightened skin, shoulder-length billowing hair, all one color, and knees that worked without encouragement. Without her consent, farming had taken its toll. But now she just wanted to hear about those tinted windows. Dotty wanted Gerard to be impressed with her own tinted windows.

"Not long ago my daughter and I, her husband, and a few other family members ventured over to Mexico. After a long sun-drenched afternoon, we waited patiently in line to cross back into the United States. One by one, we were examined and allowed to cross over.

"Then it was my turn. Suddenly my unsuspecting avocados and I were stopped. There was not much as a question or explanation. My avocados were ruefully taken from me and crudely thrown on a battered counter. But the major suspect wasn't the tasty delicacy, it was I. Shuffled into a little room, my violated avocados and I were subject to prying eyes and disbelieving ears. The powers to be were certain that my driver's license was forged, and that I was not who I proclaimed to be. I was sure they had mistaken me for a produce spy.

"Whether or not I could prove my innocence was completely up in the Mexican air. Mistakenly harboring the avocados was one thing, but being separated from the others was quite another. I was not allowed to talk to anyone about anything. For a moment, the dampness of a cold cell with tiny tinted windows surrounded me, and the smell of rottenness and filth made me sick. Who would imagine hours before, we were enjoying Cuervo Gold Margaritas ladled with olives. It was a good thing because that margarita had deadened some of my optic nerves as I watched dangling pistols pop off positioned belts. From out of nowhere, an important-looking man in full uniform walked in with an even bigger pistol dangling from his official belt. After one good look at me and my license he, pulled a knife off his belt and started skinning one of the avocados. As he jammed a small piece into his mouth, all I heard was *no bueno*. I guess I didn't pick a ripened avocado.

"Before I knew it, I was rejoined with my frantic family. A thirty-minute film on the do's and don'ts of border crossings was propped up next to one of the avocados and we were observed as we were instructed to watch every minute of it. Even today when I poke and prod an avocado for ripeness, I can still feel the tension. I still have a difficult time choosing the ripe ones but at least I have plenty of time to try.

"Border crossings are very intense places. Many tourists forget that they're entering a country with their own set of laws and procedures that must be followed to the letter. Carelessness or mistakes don't mix with borders. I guess that you learned via the film that besides avocados, it's the pit that contaminates. Parrots, parakeets, and anything with plumage or scales like iguanas are also prohibited to cross. It just takes one creature with an infection or fungus, and a resilient war would quickly escalate.

"In the United States, everything's regulated and scrutinized regarding health concerns. Not so in other countries, especially Mexico where there are no regulations and that's the problem. It's imperative that tourists be careful not only when they're leaving, but when they're entering. Except for bottled water, there's no distilled or purified water in Mexico. If you consume it in any form, it might kill you, or may cause serious damage to your system. Montezuma's revenge is just waiting for you if you forget. Lying in a prone position for a week is not uncommon if you've eaten vegetables that have been washed in the water or have mistakenly brushed your teeth with it.

"In the United States, we're so used to being protected. You'd never go into a restaurant and worry whether the food is safe to consume, but over in Mexico, you need to do just that. Eating from the street-food vendors is definitely asking for *tourista*, a sustained weekly prone position." Gerard breathed and Dotty interjected.

"Well, I guess when one crosses a border everything changes; the sights and also what happens beneath the sights. Are you involved with border security, getting monies for the new border fence and new recruitments?"

"Yes, and it's all very necessary. Have you heard of the recent exploits of United States citizens that crossed over into Mexico, yet never returned because they were trapped in a jail cell? Kidnapping and false drug accusations are rampant. Both demand enormous amounts of money to be paid to the kidnappers if there's even the slightest hope of being released.

"With the drug cartels controlling the country, bribes and illegal activity is commonplace. Mexican border agents are paid to let the drugs into and out of the country. This really is not the time to go visiting Mexico."

No one else arrived. Impatiently the guide positioned them in their seats one behind the other like in grade school. Dotty concentrated on what was seated in front of her. Gerard's arm muscles glistened in the sun as the guide's commanding oar strokes from the rear of the canoe sprayed both of them with droplets of lake water. It had been half a century since Ariel's arms looked that smooth, that taut. Without permission, age had crept up defiling her husband.

The Canadian guide spoke Canadian English with a thick French accent revealing the vivid history of the Canadian Indian tribes.

"The trading posts carried valuable buffalo skins, which the Indians made into war bonnets. The buffalo were considered a symbol of good luck. They used white eagle feathers in a broad semicircle outlined with buffalo leather with beads and buffalo horns along the sides. The war bonnets symbolized bravery and leadership within the tribe. The Sioux Indians were one of the fiercest tribes toting the most magnificent war bonnets."

Dotty could see the war bonnets swirling in the wind as the warriors clamored on horseback in search for prey: the white man, buffalo, muskrat, raccoon, and the beaver. Anything with skin, hair, or fur that could help feed or give warmth to the tribe.

The guide also pointed out natural habitats and their inhabitants. Rounding the bend, there was a perched bald eagle donned in magnificent plumage. Startled, it climbed and soared then plummeted downwards with talons outstretched grabbing an unsuspecting trout. Making a mad dash towards a nest jammed full with sticks about ten feet across, the eagle stuffed the mouths of three patient babies who cried longingly for the wiggling feast. The haunting cry from a squad of Canadian geese joined the commotion as they dipped in and out of the sunset's rays. The panoramic mountains lay partly hidden blending into the camouflaged terrain not appearing as mighty without their winter-white coating.

Abruptly, Dotty stood up and focused her camera lens at the eagle's nest. Peering through the sticks, her eyes centered on the babies' necks straining for the delicacy. Her pitched weight unbalanced the canoe.

A commanding cry filled the air, "Sit down." It was too late. Dotty toppled sideways feeling the coolness of the lake envelope her. She had not swum fully clothed since taking a lifeguard training course when she was sixteen. The lake was deep. Her feet couldn't touch the bottom. A pair of strong, muscular arms reached down and pulled her to the side of the canoe. More embarrassed than scared, Dotty felt herself hoisted up into the canoe. Jabbering in broken English and French, the horrified guide scolded her as if speaking to a little child. She deserved every word of it. What really bothered her though was her drenched camera.

Cold and crouching in the canoe, Dotty just wanted the lake cruise to end. The muscular arms in front of her lost their glamour. Her hunger took over and she just blurted out.

"Gerard, what're you going to do for dinner?" Surprised by the question, Gerard couldn't believe that shivering Dotty was thinking about dinner. But so was he. The guide's explanation about how the Indians prepared their vitals had worked up his appetite.

"We could all meet at the only available lodge. Perhaps Sara and Leon would like to join us." Gerard was now more interested. Dotty couldn't wait to get out of the canoe, call Sara, and plan their rustic dinner. The befuddled guide couldn't wait either.

THE RUSTIC AFFAIR

"Sara, is eight o'clock a good time for you and Leon to join us for dinner at the only lodge in town?"

Overhearing the invite, Leon was secretly pleased to think that Dotty and Ariel wanted to spend dinner with them.

Ariel reminded Leon of his father. When he was with him, his heart ached in a good way. He looked forward to his hardworking stories, and how he struggled. And Dotty with her easy ways, was a free gift of humor to anyone who took the time to listen. Leon listened.

Gerard had thoughts of his own. Tonight was another chance to make an impression on Sara and her needy husband. This time, he wouldn't let a spiritual water hole upstage him. If Gerard were going to intrigue, everything mattered. From the bus chit chat, Gerard recalled Sara's fondness of pink and preppy clothes. His recently pressed pink oxford button-down shirt, starched relaxed jeans, and shiny penny loafers were waiting to impress. Gerard sensed that Sara would be there with or without Leon.

Gerard was right. Before long, the five toasters celebrated their new experiences and new friendships as they sipped from goblets of brandy. The light from the roaring fireplace highlighted Sara's face. Gerard couldn't take his trained eyes off her.

Sara was pleasantly surprised to see Gerard in his shirt and loafers. *Who would dress that way for dinner in a rustic mountain lodge*, she mused. Sara was pleased to think maybe it was for her. Dotty also noticed Gerard's attention to detail and was delighted to think maybe it was for her. Earlier, Dotty mentioned how she loved the color pink, but had no idea that Gerard listened.

66

Leon couldn't take his eyes off Ariel, noticing how neatly Ariel was put together. He told him. Ariel beamed. Maybe he should listen more to his wife.

Dotty always looked her best. Usually, Ariel didn't. He worked and played in jeans. Ariel wore shirts like sneakers, over and over until his wife washed them. But tonight, he had changed his shirt and was in a pair of slacks that matched. Tonight, he was dining with the smart professor and his energetic wife. Sara moved quickly and at ninety-four Ariel was attracted to her stride.

Gerard's manners gushed with refinement. Both women couldn't help but notice. Gerard pre-ordered the wine and crystal wine goblets accompanied with chilled cheese, dip, and sesame crackers that were served on china plates encrusted with the lodge's emblem. He probably had the roaring fire re-stoked just for them.

Rustic took on a whole new meaning. Sara noticed Gerard's effect on Dotty who beamed as she talked and commented on whatever he said. Subtly Sara listened to the numerous conversations at the antique mahogany-carved dinner table. She was good at it. At school, it meant survival.

While her ears listened, her eyes wandered and latched on to another set of subtly wandering eyes. Gerard reminded Sara of the boys back in prep school who knew what to say, when to say it, and who to say it to. Quietly Gerard showed Dotty how to let her wine breathe and how to savor its aroma. Dotty would probably drink nothing but Bordeaux wine from now on just to relive the moment.

Sensing Sara's curiosity, Gerard needed to draw her in without others noticing. He was good at it. His livelihood depended on it. After all, he was a federal defense agent.

Focused, Gerard talked to the group but noted Sara's every move—how she paused, when she laughed, and why she stared. She wasn't all that easy to read. There was an underlying confusing energy about her. After sharing one of his best agent stories, Gerard was frustrated when he realized that Sara hadn't listened to most of what he had just said, so much for his department technique. Instead her eyes fastened on Ariel as he talked about farming the land. How it mattered to him. How he treated it. Gerard couldn't believe that a ninety-four-year-old man could enthrall without even trying.

Maggie was starving, and headed for the only lodge in town, hoping to run into Dave who pulled Sara out of the water hole. There were still too many unanswered questions about what happened to Sara on top of that mountain. Leon didn't seem too thrilled with Dave's explanation. I wasn't either. Courtesy is essential. Bothering guests with unwanted questions was not part of my job. I would much rather get my answers from the most reliable source and that better be Dave.

Often many of the tour directors from different tours met together for a late dinner and discussed their most unbelievable moments of the day. Tonight Maggie was sure Dave would be the center of attention. She needed to hear what actually happened without excuses. Maggie also knew that Gus knew that she would have to be very desperate to ever use him again to escort any future group up any mountain.

Opening the heavy, groaning oak door, Maggie noticed the magnificent fireplace that lit up gleaming animal eyes protruding from numerous mounted animal heads. The sight sickened her momentarily. She was not a hunter. Then in a far-back corner, she saw the colorful baseball caps huddled together, very relaxed with beer in hand. There was Dave. Posturing, Dave pulled someone or something out of a hole. Maggie was just in time and hoped she would not be disappointed. She wasn't.

"So, Dave, how did you pull her out of the ice hole? No wait, Dave, how come she was in an ice hole? I mean weren't your flags posted as to how close the viewers could get to the open holes? Didn't you test the ice before you brought them out on the ice shelf?"

Dave cringed. He expected to be entertained, not to be questioned by his peers. He wished he had never opened his mouth. Protocol wasn't followed and he knew it. Dave squirmed like a rained-on worm on a water-soaked sidewalk.

I had my answers. His embarrassment told it all. Eyes averted fumbling Dave and were drawn to Molly another tour guide, who had quickly taken over. She grabbed all the attention with an unbelievable description of a life-threatening experience.

"It all happened so quickly. Blood was everywhere. Martha was an elderly lady who traveled by herself and requested a single room. I received her call at about 10:00 p.m. and Martha complained about falling in the shower, hitting her head, and being abnormally dizzy. She felt she needed some medication to help her fall asleep and wasn't able to leave her room. I listened but my radar didn't pick up on what Martha really said. I should have heard it.

When I opened her door, Martha was lying in blood-soaked sheets, on a blood-soaked bed covering blood-soaked floorboards. It was something out of a horror movie. Shredding towels, I tried to stop the bleeding by wrapping them around her head but her hair was caked with blood. Her open gash wasn't cooperating. Martha just remained calm, too calm. She just kept asking me what to wear on the bus tomorrow. What to wear on the bus tomorrow? I couldn't believe what I heard. There might not even be a tomorrow for this lady.

Within thirty seconds, I grabbed the phone, called the ambulance, and prayed on my knees like never before. No one had ever died on one of my tours, and I wasn't going to ruin my average. Martha just apologized and hoped that she wasn't being too much of an inconvenience. She must have been in shock because her full focus was on her luggage and not wanting to leave anything behind. I tried to assure her that her things would be fine, but what I really wanted to tell her was that she might not be. But I didn't.

It was the longest and scariest ten minutes of my life. I didn't know what personal contacts to call since she had left the emergency contact slot empty on her verification form. Spying her address book on her bedside table, I quickly leafed through it and found some English addresses and phone numbers. As soon as the ambulance was on its way to the hospital, I would notify them.

Once the ambulance arrived, lifesaving medicine was administered along with properly wrapped pressure bandages, which finally stopped the bleeding. I will never forget that confused, grateful look in her eyes. It was humbling.

Peter, another guide, interrupted, "Talk about that look...I've seen it. It happened just the other day. Squished in a van, all eight of my businessmen were headed for the airport when one of the businessmen turned gray, undid his tie, and then lost everything that was inside of him on everything and anything that was beside him.

"Talk about a way to end a tour. Even though we were on the highway, he couldn't get out of that van fast enough, nor could anyone else for that matter. It looked and smelled like a war zone. The problem was that we had only a few minutes to get to the airport and couldn't wait for another van. We held our noses, and then spent the next ten minutes in the saturated van gagging on breath mints and Windex that was sprayed everywhere trying to get rid of the horrible odor.

"The sickened man was horrified, confused, and didn't know what to do. He was so grateful that I permitted him to stay in the van despite his altered appearance and intoxicating odor. He would have to wait and get cleaned up once he got to the airport. I just didn't have the heart to make him wait for another van. How could I? I mean, he didn't plan on getting sick. To be honest with you, even if he hadn't felt well it wouldn't have really made any difference. We were on the freeway and couldn't have just pulled over. It was just so surreal, but as tour directors, we have to be prepared for anything."

Maggie jumped in.

"We need to be prepared, but so do our tourists once the tour is over. The mental adjustment after the tour can be just as disarming as any physical ailments.

"You're no longer told when to eat, where to eat, what to eat, when to sleep, where to sleep, and when to get up. On the tour, every minute of everyday you're told what to do and how to do it and often it's extremely difficult to deprogram oneself mentally.

"Just last week, I'll never forget when I dropped off numerous couples at the last hotel for their last overnight stay. The next day was a free day being the day of departure. When I reappeared in the morning to pick up evaluations and collect my tips, I couldn't believe that it was the same group. Many of the individuals whom I talked with seemed to be having a difficult time functioning and were only concerned about the time. They certainly had one priority straight.

"To top it off, the dining room at the hotel was being refurbished and no one knew where to go for breakfast or how to get there. It was pandemonium. Many forgot how to reason, how to think.

"Some of them just refused and waited for me to intervene, but I didn't. Their deprogramming needed to get started, and I needed to get to the airport. Looking back, I saw confused and grateful faces, wondering what came next."

Word of mouth meant everything in our business and I think Dave already got what he deserved, self-degradation in front of beer-toting peers. If his phone rang at all, it wouldn't be for any glacial tours. Looking around, I took a mental head count of contented diners.

I couldn't help but notice the group—the professor, his wife, the farmers from California, and the agent from Washington. It was a good political mix and I wished I were at the table sharing the colorful conversation. Bouts of laughter surrounded them. Their eyes twinkled, lighting up any harbor. I wonder if they knew? My mind was already thinking about tomorrow's much-anticipated ferry ride over to Vancouver Island. I decided to scoot over to the lights and breathe in some of that needed laughter.

"Sara, Leon, how great it is to see you enjoying yourselves. How was your dinner?"

The quality of their food and their service was very important to me. It would be on their evaluation form and my tips would reflect it one way or the other.

"Maggie, please join us for a nightcap. Everything was delightful," spoken from a mouth of a contented guest. That was all that I needed to hear before a snifter of almond brandy saturated my waiting taste buds.

Gerard definitely was the center of attention as Dotty and even Sara clung to his every other word. I guess an agent was alluring in a way, but I preferred the hallowed halls and found it hard to keep my eyes off the professor. Ariel was my competition, so I redirected my gaze to the wall and latched on to a set of soft, mounted brown eyes that reaffirmed what I was supposed to be thinking about: tonight's accommodations and tomorrow's ferry.

THE CHARMING HERON

efore we got to the ferry, Gus insisted that we go over bus rules: how and when to unload and reload the bus. Ears listened attentively while mouths munched on not-quite-finished oatmeal bars and assorted doughnuts. Like bats, the smell of coffee hung in the air. The permanent smell of spilled coffee didn't please anyone, especially Gus since he had to clean it up.

"You'll disembark carefully from the bus once we get to the wharf at the unloading station. Make sure that you take a good look at the bus before you leave because if you can't identify it, you won't get back on it. Once you disembark from the bus, you'll be herded into small groups with other tourists from other tours.

"Before anyone is allowed on the ferry, every individual is searched and sniffed by aggressive dogs. So if you're not accustomed to noisy German shepherds, get ready. Lately there hasn't been any nipped skin reported."

I gave Gus one of my looks. He usually didn't add that last statement and I certainly didn't see the humor in it. He knew that I wasn't pleased and toned it down.

"If you see many buses being loaded on the ferry, don't be concerned. There's a weight limit and reservations are made, in advance. There are just so many buses and so many passengers permitted on each ferry according to the weigh-in. Not one more. Not one less."

"Are the passengers weighed as well?" chomped an oversized Englishman all decked out in his maritime best.

Some concerned faces were turned towards me so I continued, "No, there's no personal weigh-in, but the only thing that really does need to fit is the life jacket that they give you when you board. Tie it and try it is what I always suggest just to be sure."

"As you board, you'll also be given a map of the ferry since it has three decks, two restaurants, two shops, an elevator, and multistepped stairs. If you like fresh air and openness, the best ride is on the top deck. If you don't want to get too windblown, a covered deck would be a better choice. Once on the ferry, you may roam freely. Pay attention to the roped-off areas. Don't get too close to the edge of the railings. Enjoy the beautiful scenery especially the birds and if we're lucky, we might even be privy to a playful pod of humpback whales."

The concerned looks now relaxed, ready for fun, ready to be sniffed. Gus and I have done this hundreds of times but invariably there was always the possibility of a mishap. Some of the tourists might get back splashed from the ferry's tremendous wake. Maybe get disoriented for a moment or two when the ferry started up and perhaps lose their footing. Maybe even be mistaken for a bird refuge as the seabirds were famous for their precision droppings on the upper deck.

The bus quickly unloaded and the group was assimilated by throngs of eager passengers. The German shepherds seemed frisky, but everyone sailed through the search without incident. I never had a tourist detained for drugs or carrying a weapon. I was not about to tarnish my record.

"Maggie, it looks good. Everyone got on, the bus has been tucked away, and I'm ready for some clam chowder and oyster crackers. Can I get you anything?"

Gus knew. He usually couldn't wait to get away from me and mingle with the other bus drivers. After a quick lunch, the drivers would each head back to their individual buses and get at least an hour nap.

"Gus, I can't explain it. It isn't anything physical so I guess. It's, well, I guess it's the ferry, it just doesn't feel right to me."

"Maggie, how many times have we done this? We could do it blindfolded if we had to. What does it feel like?"

Gus was well aware that I was stressed out over Dave and his antics. This was definitely not the same confident Maggie that was in complete control of the bus just thirty minutes ago.

"I know this sounds strange, but it's as if the ferry knows something that it shouldn't. I don't know if it's the weight, the number of buses, or the tours that are here. Just look around. This ferry is jam-packed."

"Maggie, I've never mentioned this before, but I always make it a point to personally check the weighing scale not just for our bus, but also for the other buses and their cargos. It interests me. You may find it hard to believe but this ferry isn't even at its full weight limit capacity. I think there's room for one more bus."

Sometimes Gus could really calm my nerves and now was one of those times. As quickly as the feeling surfaced, it faded.

"Gus, whatever it was, left. Go find your buddies, and I'll meet you back at the bus in about two hours." As Gus disappeared in the many faces, the sounds of the waves washing up against the boat transfixed me. Sleepily, I yielded for a brief moment. I closed my tired eyes. The uneasiness drifted away.

Sara couldn't wait to get on that ferry. The hour bus ride to the ferry had already been too much for her. She wasn't accustomed to drinking anything except cranberry juice or milk with dinner, maybe a glass of Zinfandel on a special occasion.

Last night set a new record for her and she didn't need to count. The food was wonderful. The company was divine, something totally unexpected. Being with Dotty and Ariel was fairly interesting and fun but being with Gerard was exceptionally interesting and much more than fun.

Gerard was gracious. Sara couldn't help but respond. Breathing slowly, Sara was thankful for salty ocean air, a soft breeze, and the chance to sort things out.

She had left Leon down below in the covered deck sitting contentedly on a comfortable chair eating a bowl of shrimp, basking in the frenzy around him.

Food distracted Sara. After she moved away from the hungry crowd, things began to make more sense especially when the covered deck over her head disappeared.

Clutching her binoculars, Sara searched the ocean for any black-tipped fins and then made a quick overhead circle for her birds. Sara was not disappointed. There was a magnificent blue heron that landed nearby on some mounds of seaweed. It basked in the sun, pecking bits of plumage that was matted down by the salty water.

"It's quite a showstopper, isn't it?" She heard from behind her. The voice sounded very familiar. Her face flushed. She only hoped that he couldn't read minds or sense what she had been thinking about——his permeating charm. That made her blush all the more.

"You need some sunscreen on your cheeks. Here let me apply it for you." Sara was so embarrassed that she almost lost the little composure that remained. Suddenly the ferry lurched forward as if part of a script. Sara lost her footing tumbling into Gerard's outstretched arms.

"Don't worry, I have you," was all she heard as she looked into confident eyes. Just then a brilliant ray of sunlight cascaded down on her wedding ring and it sparkled as never before.

"Last night was such a nice dinner. Everyone seemed to really enjoy themselves. It wasn't too over the top was it? I mean with all the brandy, wine, and after-dinner cordials? Coffee was a definite must this morning. Am I right?"

Gerard paused and got serious.

"Did Leon at least get some temporary relief from that badgering pain in his leg?" As if rehearsed, Gerard knew just what to say. Sara was anything but rehearsed and didn't have the right words.

"Dinner was wonderful. Back home in Connecticut, an after-dinner tradition was a brandy snifter with a sugar-coated rim just like we had it last night. Since you're from Washington, DC, I guess maybe it's an East Coast favorite because they certainly don't drink brandy in Texas. Maybe it doesn't get cold enough."

Right then, Gerard looked through her, and Sara wondered if he took anything from her except her disorganized thoughts.

"Maybe it's just too hot in Texas and they don't know how to relax. I know a few Texans and they sure are hyper. They just don't know when to be quiet."

"After fifteen years, I'm now considered one of them. Sometimes Leon asks me to go outside because I make him nervous."

"Sara, I think your energy level is due more to school. I've never met a calm teacher. It's probably not permitted."

"Have you done much traveling? What a golden opportunity for you with your summers off and all."

"A few summers ago, I traveled alone to a painting paradise––Europe. It has been my favorite tour so far, a different world, a different time, a different pace. Once you got off the plane, there really wasn't any pace.

"In France, the French ate when they got hungry regardless of the hour. On our tour, dinner was served at nine o'clock. Oddly enough, we became accustomed to late lunches and late dinners.

"As we viewed the French follies, the pace quickened. There were a few individuals that were unfamiliar with them and were quite shocked by the dancers' behavior. They spent the entire evening in the back of the French theatre persuading one another not to look because of the scanty clothing, if any, was worn at all. I was one of them."

Gerard's heart skipped a couple of beats as he remembered Venice. If only Sara had been with him.

"I don't know about France, but in Venice time stopped," Gerard reminisced. "Being serenaded on the gondola...it was very Italian."

Sara's face lit up as she also remembered the gondoliers' spell.

"I fell in love with each and every one of them especially when they were singing 'Volare.'" Gerard was back on the gondola swishing through the canals and reached for Sara's hand. It wasn't there.

"Do you remember the marketplace where easels swooped down on you? Grabbing your attention, every artist's fiery stroke fixated you. The Italian sky wasn't painted first but last. It was so real that you could almost feel the sun's rays and shadows. Churches etched in stained glass colors waved their crosses proudly while gondolas floated in the distance."

How could Sara ever forget those churches? St. Peter's Basilica had a magnificent dome and stained glass masterpieces throughout. The awe muffled you as you walked in. The grandeur of the statues and pedestals throughout the church's inner sanctum was done in such detail and reverence. The angels with every hand, every eye, every mouth, and every set of wings were intricately sculptured.

"The Italians also had fiery tempers. I'll never forget when we were in the Sistine Chapel that everyone was instructed to be quiet, but this one Italian couple didn't oblige and just kept on talking. All of us were transfixed with its ceiling: those fingers, those angels and demons fighting for souls. One couldn't help but be drawn to the reverence, the quietness.

"The instructions were given in English, so I thought the Italian couple didn't understand so I motioned to the couple to be quiet. The woman erupted. It was volcanic, a highly toxic outburst that didn't stop. I was so glad that I couldn't understand a word of it. But her face was another matter, twisting and turning. I have not tried to quiet anyone since."

Sara couldn't wait any longer. "Was this the bus tour that started in England and traveled through France, Switzerland, and Italy?"

"The very one. So you're familiar with it?"

"Familiar, with every breath on that bus tour I became European. England was one of my favorite countries. Landing in London, I couldn't help but notice the differences right away.

"It was near noon so we went to high tea, which was filled with porcelain teacups, yummy delicacies, and lots of etiquette. From there, we mounted the trams that could take you anywhere and lose you everywhere. The English could see a stranded tourist at least a mile away and were always polite, helping you decipher the signs knowing just how to get you back on track.

"We toured the castles, the moats, the lookout towers, and visualized the knights of armor knee-deep in battle. The richness of the queen's castle with matching décor in every room, the blue room, the green room, all the different colored rooms that represented royal pedigrees and designated activities for visiting monarchs and heads of state. Crystal chandeliers dripped of elegance and grandeur. The queen's crowns and jewels were all under lock and key, but accessible to the prying public like me.

"I went up and down the rows of encased crowns many times. I just couldn't get enough of those walnut-sized emeralds, sapphires, and diamonds. It was a thief's fantasy," Sara continued reliving her trip.

"Our accommodations were not a fantasy by any means. My bed was so short that my feet hung over the ends, and the room was so tiny that there wasn't really a left or right side, everything was just in front of you. I didn't dare turn around in the shower for fear of banging into a wall. When turning on the water, you had to be careful that you didn't flood the entire bathroom since the drain was slow, half clogged up and right in the middle of the floor. One night, I did exactly that and was lucky that I didn't leave any of my luggages on the floor. It would have been ruined.

"The English always looked so tall, so rested, so clean, and so crisp. I still haven't quite figured out how they did it. I don't remember ever seeing an ironing board tucked away, but then I never looked for one. The clothes, outfits, and colors, always matched. They breathed fashion and the simpler the better. The women wore their suits and sandals on the trains with a pair of high heels tucked under their arms. Reading, they always had their nose in a book or the newspaper. Their stops were memorized, and they never even looked up when they got off. The English reeked of independence and culture."

Gerard remembered.

"Even in the shops, the English were very courteous. I got some tailored dress shirts, which were tailored for me exclusively at a very small, yet elegant shop, which was hidden away almost completely out of view. Often when you take your time, you can make some wonderful finds."

Sara agreed, "I'll never forget the find that I made in Switzerland. I was looking for a Swiss watch and couldn't find one. Much to my surprise, a small store way off the beaten path had exactly what I wanted. The owner was very Swiss, equally as delightful and gift wrapped the watch for me at no added expense.

"Switzerland was contagious. Everywhere you went, snowcapped mountains and flowering hills gazed at you. In a gondola that slowly ascended its way up the yellow-and-purple-flowered mountainside, I watched a worn goat herder herd his stubborn goats with the help of a shaggy sheepdog. Cow bells clanged in the distance." Listening to Sara made Gerard want to return.

"The goat herders lived in little shacks with makeshift chimneys that dotted the hills. In town, the cobblestone streets were filled with tulip-covered windowsills, wonderful singsong enunciations, and world-renowned chocolates.

"I remembered that the Swiss enjoyed doing things their own way in their own time. I stayed at a small Swiss chalet on Lake Lucerne that donned the authentic Swiss icing along the roof with a frame as its base. On a hill high above the chalet sat the town's church complete with a towering steeple and chiming clock that serenaded you every hour. Can you imagine being awoken by Alpine chimes every morning? I was for four lingering days." As Sara spoke, Gerard listened to the chimes.

"Sara, I hope you were able to take the cruise on Lake Lucerne. Covering the lakeside were multimillion dollar properties that were hardly ever used. Many served as beautifully manicured tax shelters for the well-heeled. Our guide pointed out *summer cottages* owned by famous movie stars and chief executive officers (CEOs) who visited only in the summer if at all.

"There were many pristine sights but the most stirring thing I saw was the huge statuesque lion who was dedicated to all of the soldiers who had died in the Swiss wars. With its towering granite backdrop, the spouting lion reflected its sprawling torso and giant paws below in the waters that surrounded it. Honor and self-respect clung to it as if on guard, the lion watched overhead as people tossed in coins and whispered quietly." Gerard could still see those outstretched paws.

"Gerard, I didn't have a chance to take that Lucerne cruise, but it sure sounds lovely. But one of our first stops in Switzerland was viewing that lion. If you looked closely, there was a single tear carved into the lion's cheek that continually filled with water as the lion gushed rivulets of water. It was powerful. It made you think."

"Sara, I've been thinking. Since Leon doesn't like to travel and my fiancée doesn't have the time to travel perhaps..."

"Perhaps." Sara let her guard down. From tumbling into Gerard's arms, and gazing at his stealthy, traveled eyes, she was still mentally swaying from last night's charm.

"Sara, one more thing, I hope we can share another night like last night." With that last remark, Gerard slowly turned away and vanished just like the charming blue heron.

Back on the lower deck, Ariel's farmer antics reminded Leon of his happy-go-lucky dad. Ariel was good-natured, and nothing bruised him except maybe the weather and Dotty's stubborn knees. Leon was bruised. Divorced and raising two feisty daughters, he knew all too well how easily it could happen.

Leon dreaded this three-hour ferry ride especially since Sara was nowhere in sight and there wasn't anyone to help him. But all that changed in an instant when Ariel and Dotty sat down beside him. Leon was grateful. Time passed quickly around Ariel. The three hours turned into a relaxed therapy session with Leon laughing more than Ariel. He seldom laughed and had forgotten its carefree sound.

"Well, look what the wind blew in," commented Ariel as Gerard sat done casually pushing away some soup bowls.

"It's really blowing up on the top deck, so I thought I'd come down and warm up."

"We could all use a snifter of last night's warm brandy right about now," laughed Ariel as Leon readjusted himself trying to get comfortable.

"Leon, how's that pain today?" asked windblown Gerard.

"Well, the water, just being near it, the dampness and humidity brings on the phantom pain. The doctors keep telling me it's all in my mind, but I still feel every bit of it."

"Not too long ago, I saw a documentary on phantom pain and it showed how, if you followed the limb down to where it should be and massaged the area, the pain would lessen," suggested Gerard.

"Yes, I saw the same one, a case of mental gymnastics." Sara tried it, massaging my missing right foot then my missing right leg. It seemed to work for a while. Then the pain returned with a vengeance. It's difficult to explain phantom pain when it doesn't even make sense."

"Ariel, tell Leon and Gerard about your date with pain."

"About four years ago, my chest hurt off and on, and then one day, I couldn't sit up and run the tractor. Dotty called an ambulance and within twenty-four hours, I had four new arteries. It could have gone either way the doctor said. I just wasn't being careful looking for the signs. Today, when I'm in pain, I take care of it."

"Four arteries, is that all?" interrupted Leon. "Seven years ago, I just didn't feel right and refused to leave the hospital until they gave me a complete checkup from head to toe. I had every kind of test imaginable and it's a good thing because they found six of my arteries were nonfunctioning. I was perfect fatal heart attack material. Two days later, I had six new arteries, a scar from my upper chest to my waist, a calf-length leg scar, a very thankful family, and a very stressed out wife. Ariel, did you know that our hearts now are as good as twenty year olds?"

"Leon, I'm sure glad to know that statistic. Maybe Dotty will let me speed it up a bit."

"Personally, I'm more familiar with backs than hearts since my fiancée is a chiropractor," stated Gerard. "Talk about speed, I can hardly keep up with her. I want to encourage her practice but often it interferes. Gwena was suppose to accompany me on this trip but then at the very last minute declined after I had made all the reservations. Too many backs had to be readjusted and aligned. She just didn't want to let her patients down. It's hard to rely on these professional women. Often they don't have time for their own lives."

"Look over to our right. It's land, mates, Vancouver Island." Sara quickly came down the stairs joining the spirited group.

"Are we there yet?" Sara teased as she put her arm around Leon who was glad that she was back near him. Feeling guilty about her preoccupation with Gerard, Sara actually helped Leon, partly propping him up as they headed for the bus.

Vancouver Island was directly in front of us. Refreshed, I was ready to escort the group back to the bus. I didn't have to. Gus was way ahead of me and everyone seemed to be anchored back in their assigned seat. Sara was already doing a head count, pure instinct she couldn't help it. So I followed suit: The British group had visited some of the ferry's shops and were toting insignia towels and hats. The Israeli honeymooners were still gazing longingly at one another with ferry mist in their eyes. The Australians donned matching Victoria T-shirts and looked ready for the island. The Japanese couples had been shopping as well and crammed some just-purchased bathing suits and pairs of sneakers under their spacious seat.

Last night's dinner group was tired but content, and Gerard was by Leon's side helping him up the bus steps. We reached Victoria without any mishaps. That unsettling feeling didn't return. That extra cup of coffee was probably way too much caffeine for me.

The Queen Victoria Hotel was only thirty minutes away on the other side of the island close to the harbor. I wanted to get everyone in their assigned rooms before dinner time so if I made any changes, there would be plenty of time. Victoria was a place for exploring, plenty of eateries, and quaint restaurants for those who had not opted for dinner in the hotel. The extra time was helpful.

THE PINK FISH

||||||||||||||||||||||||||||||||||||||||||||||||||||||||||||||||||||||||||||||||||||||||||||||||||||||||||||||||||||||||||||||||||||||||||

We were ready for the hotel, but the hotel was not ready for us. Sometimes that happened when a large group or convention got a courtesy of a late check out. There were always stragglers and that was the problem. When tourists can't check into their rooms, they are unhappy especially after three hours on a ferry however exciting it was.

I didn't need to look at the faces for verification. I felt the looks. Ultimately, I was responsible for any check-in problems. This one took me completely by surprise. Usually food can soften anyone at any time. The maitre d' and I were on the same wavelength as bottles of champagne appeared out of the Victorian air. Eyes celebrated as tops popped and glasses clanged. Within minutes, quite an assortment of cheese and shrimp followed.

By the time our rooms were ready, no one cared. Most were just as happy in the lobby and found elegant lounging areas to their liking. In fact, they didn't want to leave. Encouraging them, I called out their rooms and handed them their individual keys.

A few elderly couples needed to have a room change because they were too tired to climb the stairs and didn't have the steady patience for the elevator. I already switched Dr. Angel's room to a suite since Sara informed me that he would be spending a lot of the time in his room and we would be here for four days.

Tonight the hotel served smoked salmon in one of the dining areas that was assigned to our group. The salmon was always fresh. That was one thing I didn't have to worry about. When the harbor and fishing boats could be seen from the dining room window, you knew the fish came right off the hooks. Dinner was served at seven in the evening so there was plenty of time to enjoy the champagne's aftermath.

I tried to allow some free time before dinner. Some chose formal dress and some casual dress. Sometimes I hardly recognized the guests cleaned up and polished like best silver.

Tonight I would be dining in the hotel. The salmon smelled terrific. I was hungry. There wasn't time for me to indulge in champagne, so I was more than ready for dinner. At dinner, the diners sat where they wanted. I can't even remember the last time that I had assigned seating at the dinner tables. The bus was enough. I didn't want a revolt in my hands.

Making a mental checklist of those who signed up for the dinner, I saw that Leon sat close to the entrance. Where was Sara? Maybe she was running late.

"Leon, do I need to hold Sara's dinner for her?"

"No, Maggie, that won't be necessary. Sara needed to go out and get rid of some of her energy. So I think she, Dotty, and Ariel opted to explore."

"The three of them should find plenty out there for dinner options. Are you comfortable sitting here? Would you like to join another couple?"

"No, Maggie, I'm fine. I'm a bit tired and not really very talkative."

"Would you mind if I joined you? I'll do most of the talking." I laughed and wasn't sure if I was welcome or not.

"That'd be nice, Maggie. I'd like to hear all about this island, what's noteworthy."

"Leon, this island has so many things tucked out of view. Yet others are very much in view. Take for instance the harbor with its international fishing trade. Boats from all over the world are welcome here. Just this weekend, there's a hundred-and-fifty-foot yacht, The World Tour, moored in the harbor that has yachtsmen working on it from all over the world. If you look closely you can see flags representing each country flapping along the halyards all along the top of the boat and on its sides. You just have to see this phenomenon and hear the accents that weave in and out like a concert's musical instruments.

"The Empress Hotel is another sight that you can't possibly miss. Steeped in its British Victorian roots, the hotel was built using chalet architecture and traditional elegance. If you didn't know any better, you might think you were back in England, in a royal chalet on the Thames

River. Tomorrow maybe it might be fun to have a famous cup of tea in their classic dining room. I'll probably have some free time about noon." I wanted to look straight into Leon's eyes but I didn't have to. He was looking straight into mine.

"Maggie, are you asking me out?"

I could feel my face flush. "Well, maybe, not exactly, it'd just be fun."

"It's okay, Maggie, I just wanted to see your face match your outfit. I'll check with Sara and am sure she'll think it's a great idea. So it's tomorrow then."

"The Empress Hotel's dining room is a little pricy. The atmosphere makes up for it. Tour directors get a substantial discount so you'll be my guest.

"There are elegant shops for every taste. The nice feature about shopping here's that you can ship everything home, so that you don't have to worry about losing or breaking it. Not far from the Empress Hotel is the Parliament building, which at night is lit up like a holiday scene on a Christmas card." Maggie was really good at drawing people in.

"The Parliament may or may not be in session. Tours are offered during the day and you can actually sit in or listen in on the proceedings. Notably, security is tight but it has to be."

Just then there was a horrible gagging sound two tables down from us. I jumped up and couldn't get there fast enough.

Mr. Hieto, one of my Japanese tourists, was very white in the face, gagging and sagging in his chair. His wife was beside herself, jabbering Japanese and waving her hands throughout the air as though in a mantra. My instinct said choking, but Mr. Franco, who sat right behind him, had already given him a few sharp blows on the back and nothing popped out. Mr. Hieto kept pointing to the fish, muttering. Confused, I grabbed a napkin and stuffed it with ice trying to hold it near his forehead.

"Maggie, it's food poisoning. He needs to be rushed to the hospital, or he'll never make it." I turned around and Gerard had already called an ambulance. But how could he have known? Gerard didn't even sign up for dinner, but had decided to venture down. I was so thankful that he did.

Within minutes, Mr. Hieto was strapped on the stretcher, ready for the mad dash to the hospital. His wife knew that something was very wrong and kept pointing to the pink fish and sobbing. Another Japanese couple was trying to translate what Mrs. Hieto said in between sobs. Her husband usually spoke for her, and she wasn't accustomed to drama, or having to explain herself.

"Tell her that I'm taking her husband to the hospital where they'll take care of him and get rid of the pink fish." Mrs. Hieto suddenly got very brave, got up and also strapped herself into the seat of the ambulance. No pink fish was going to take her husband away from her. She didn't budge. The ambulance was big enough for the other couple as well and I needed a translator. We all piled in. The attendants were already trying to get Mr. Hieto to dislodge some of the deadly fish.

I never had anyone have an allergic reaction to the food before. Prior to putting one foot on that bus, every single guest had to fill out a sheet documenting any medicine, food, or toxin that they were allergic to.

Every morning on the bus, each guest was given a menu and food selections were made for the entire day. If substitutions were needed, they were made then and there. Mr. Hieto must have overlooked the salmon. He still looked white as sea-foam and I wasn't sure what to expect.

The attendants inserted an IV into Mr. Hieto and gave him some awful-smelling medicine to counteract the swallowed fish. It did. I doubt whether I will ever eat salmon again.

Before you could say pink salmon, the lights of the emergency room welcomed us. Mr. Hieto and his entourage were ushered into a room as the last determined bits of fish were removed. He was going to make it. Mrs. Hieto couldn't be more gracious. She pulled herself out of her mantra and bobbed up and down like a cork, thanking everyone in Japanese.

Back at the hotel's dining room, Leon couldn't believe his eyes.

"Gerard, I don't know how you do it, but I'm glad that you do," Leon quietly said as he looked closely at Gerard. Nope, there were no wings.

"I just thought that I'd come down and visit with you. I noticed that Sara took off with Dotty and Ariel."

"How did you know about Mr. Hieto? You seemed so sure."

"I've seen food poisoning before: the loss of color, the sagging, even foaming at the mouth. It has seizure like symptoms. It's imperative to get the toxin out before it kills the victim. Mr. Hieto is a lucky man. Not a good way to clear a restaurant."

Leon looked around and an uncertain quietness lingered. Many had left. The waiters were busy boxing up the dinners. Leon made sure that Maggie's dinner was boxed up as well.

"Leon, let's give the bar some business. What about a nightcap?"

Leon normally didn't drink two nights in a row, but he couldn't get Mr. Hieto's face out of his mind and he wanted to.

"A brandy, like we had last night?" Gerard knew Leon's leg was not cooperating. He could see it in his face. Brandy was a snifter of liquid aspirin.

"Here's to Mr. Hieto, never eating salmon again," quipped Gerard as Leon's face relaxed.

"Maggie and I are scheduled for a cup of tea at the Empress Hotel tomorrow at noon. I just need to get Sara's okay."

"You're going to check with Sara first?"

"Sure, it's just an outing. I mean Maggie is a certified tour director. What better company could you ask for?"

"I guess you have a point there. But won't Sara mind you going without her?"

"Are you kidding me? When we first were married I had several professional outings at the college that I needed to attend. Sara never wanted to go. Most of my peers don't even really believe that there is a Sara. They have never met her."

Gerard was completely caught off guard. For once he didn't have a reply. None of it made any sense. Did Leon really know anything about his wife? He needed to find out.

"Why don't you join us? It should be fun. How can you not have fun with a gal like Maggie? She's fiery, energetic, smart, and enjoys elegant tea and scones. What do you think?" Gerard wasn't thinking about anything except Sara and why she never went anywhere with her husband. He would go. It would give him a chance to find some answers.

Sara couldn't believe her eyes. It was Christmas time without the snow. Dripped in little white lights The Parliament building shouted out its magnificence. You couldn't take your eyes off of it. Spellbound, Sara waited for Dotty and Ariel.

"It would look nice on a Christmas card, one of my hand-painted cards that the local stores buy back home," replied Dotty. "It's a contingency agreement. I paint at least one hundred cards for the holidays and make a fixed amount on each purchased card. It helps provide a merry Christmas."

Sara's respect for Dotty charged ahead.

"I paint with oils, mostly landscapes but haven't sold any as yet. Usually I give them to my mother who has decorated a portion of her house with them."

"Well, I paint equipment, run down equipment that looks as though the life were kicked out of it. Once I get a coat of paint on, it lifts up its head and is ready to go harvest another wheat field or garnish fruit in the orchards."

"Ariel, you're right. Appearance matters. It's an attitude. It's contagious."

Their attitudes couldn't be more contagious. They were relaxed and ready for a Mexican fiesta.

When the trio returned to the hotel, attitudes changed. Conversations regarding Mr. Hieto debated whether or not he would be eulogized or be joining them for tomorrow's festivities. With all the frenzy, Sara didn't really understand what happened until she got back to her suite. The smell of fish hit her in the face as soon as she walked in the room. It was salmon, a smell that she didn't care for. It had to be Leon's dinner leftovers that needed to be picked up by room service. Sara noticed that the fish was all wrapped up.

Before she could find out about the fish, Leon intoxicated her with the events about Mr. Hieto and his allergic reaction. Horrified, Sara was so glad that she wasn't there. She wasn't good with drama and fell apart. What about Maggie? She had no idea that being a tour director was such a responsibility. Life and death all because of one smelly pink fish.

"Sara, that's Maggie's dinner that she never had a chance to eat. Would you call room service and see if they'd deliver it to her room?"

"By the way, Maggie invited me and Gerard for high tea tomorrow. After all of tonight's antics, she probably needs to unload a bit. Who better to be with than us?"

Sara was happy that Leon was going to actually get out of the suite and go somewhere especially with Maggie and Gerard who both deserved a fisherman's trophy after tonight.

"Tomorrow I'm going to go explore the out-of-view places via the park that we passed and hopefully find a way down to the rocky beach."

"Sara, you know how I promised your mother that I wouldn't let you go off by yourself."

"I won't be alone. Don't worry. There'll be throngs of tourists all over the place. The islanders are used to them and probably wouldn't even consider giving you the time of day."

Sara couldn't wait for tomorrow when she would be alone and able to think her own thoughts. Little did she know how truly alone she would be.

A WHALER'S DELIGHT

||||||||||||||||||||||||||||||||||||||||||||||||||||||||||||||||||||||||||||||||||||||||||||||||||||||||||||||||||||||||||||||||||||||||||||||||||||||

T he clock urged me to get up. After my long evening, it was way too early way too soon. Today we were off to the sea again, but this time looking for whales. I instructed the twenty-five whale seekers to be ready to leave by seven thirty. It would take us about fifteen minutes to get to the wharf and get loaded on the boat.

At least this excursion didn't involve any type of meal. After Mr. Hieto fully recovered, he and his wife would rejoin the group. Earlier, the smell of salmon saturated me; my hair, skin, and clothes. Scrubbing with lavender soap and dosing myself with French perfume didn't mask it.

Everything was in order as I rechecked the expiration dates on the credit card vouchers for the whaling excursion. Whaling would be a welcome diversion after last night. Tea with the professor would be an even better diversion and crossed my mind more than once. Hopefully Sara would allow Leon to join me and have some fun. I counted on it.

The bus was Gus-less, which was unusual but it gave me time to check the binoculars and make sure that they worked. The cruise ship would have its own binoculars for a fee, but I tried to distribute mine to those who would really use them and didn't want to pay for them. Often it was the two-dollar fees that would fuel the guests' anger on those evaluation forms, so I tried to present options. Options kept a tour director alive.

When touring, some guests wanted the best of the best regardless of the price whether it be a choice of hotel rooms, restaurants, or activities. If conditions were right, helicopter rides, river rafting, and seaplane excursions all needed to be available. Customers might spend five hundred dollars on a helicopter ride and refuse to pay two dollars for a snapshot. Everyone perceived things differently. It was my job to anticipate the perceptions.

"Maggie, sorry I'm a little late, but I thought after last night that you would probably be a little late yourself." I hated excuses and Gus knew it.

"Mr. Hieto has recovered, and I just finished checking the binoculars," as Gus listened to Maggie, he thought it was always work, never having any fun together. "I'll make an announcement regarding Mr. Hieto once everyone arrives."

"Any wait at the hospital?" Gus asked. "You certainly don't look like you've been up half the night. Maggie, if there's anything that I can do for you, let me know." As usual, Gus tried to be very nice when he didn't need to be. It just wasn't necessary. Right now we had whalers to be concerned about and whether they would be ready on time. As if a loudspeaker gathered them up, they all suddenly appeared out of nowhere. The first words out of their mouths were, "How was Mr. Hieto?"

"It was a long night at the emergency room, but we got there in plenty of time and Mr. Hieto received excellent care. By now I'm sure he has achieved celebrity status among the Vancouver fisherman knowing how he survived their prized delicacy. He'll probably need a day to recover. He and his wife should rejoin the group later."

When two individuals from the group weren't there, it was noticed. There were many foreigners in the group. Many were very far from home and were very relieved that it didn't happen to them.

As I passed out the binoculars, some extra reassuring words were needed. I needed to get them ready for whale sighting in the ocean. Everyone who was on the list was accounted for, well, almost everyone. Gerard walked quickly around the corner. He was never late. He looked calm and cool just like last night. The government trained him well.

"Good morning, Maggie," Gerard casually offered as he passed me. "Last night Mr. Hieto couldn't have been in better hands. I trust we'll see him later on in the day."

Gerard looked as though he had something on his mind other than Mr. Hieto. I didn't want to bother his intensity.

The whale watchers needed to know something about the different types of whales that they might see. Briefly, I went into my whaling speech and was harpooned in the middle of it. Gus added a few stories and personal adages to heighten the anticipation. It worked and within fifteen minutes, it was a different group, focused now on seeing as many whales as possible.

When we arrived, we first stopped at one of the oldest canneries on the coast, the North Pacific Cannery in Port Edward. We then boarded our ferry and continued on headed toward Prince Rupert and on to the Queen Charlotte Islands. Everything was so regal on the water especially the names. The channels near Prince Rupert were encased by snow-covered mountains and were part of the archipelago which led on to the Queen Charlotte Sound.

"Maggie, nine o'clock," shouted Gerard. It was the first sighted whale, a gray humpback. It couldn't get high enough out of the water. What a sight for searching eyes. Cameras couldn't keep up as individuals dodged this way and that to get the perfect picture. Gerard certainly never missed anything. It was a good thing or last night could have been deadly. Thankful, I needed to tell him. Edging over toward Gerard, I caught his eye.

"Last night, Gerard, I was certainly grateful for your insight. Your quick thinking really made a difference to all of us."

"Maggie, I was just glad to be able to identify the culprit."

The ladies from Australia had spotted something.

"Maggie, what kind of whale is that?" asked Sharman, one of the New Zealand widowers, gasping in awe as the whale shoved his head out of the water.

"It's an orca," commented Gerard, overhearing the question. He knew his whales. Did he know his birds?

"Let's keep a lookout for birds also since we're in the Pacific Flyway. Many of the migrating birds come in the winter; to relax, eat, and end up staying for a season. Others stay for the winter then head on to California and Mexico completely refreshed. Summer is breeding season, so we should see plenty of courtship: singing, displaying, and nesting."

"What about that beauty at six o'clock; can anyone identify it?" My dad instilled in me the love of birds as well as buses and I knew them by heart.

"I believe it's the Eurasian wigeon," offered Gerard. Glancing quickly at his hands, I was certain he had a bird book. I was wrong. He saw the surprised look on my face. "Birds are one of my passions. They're so unregulated and have such interesting habits––so unlike people."

"Maggie, was Gerard right?" inquired Sharman, her eyes lit up brightly.

"Yes, that's exactly it."

"There are some honking geese at two o'clock. Haunting and surreal, there was nothing quite like being on the water at sundown and having the night air filled with the geese's insistent honking.

"The trumpeter swan is another bird of song that gathers at sundown, but is much more musical. A flock of swans sounds like taps vibrating through the air. Up ahead is a bird sanctuary where they take care of injured falcons and birds of prey. If we had more time, we could stop."

"Maggie, I never knew there would be so many birds. What I wouldn't give to see a bald eagle. I've heard how regal they are with their white-feathered heads and black six-foot wingspans," commented Zanna, the Israeli honeymooner. She now seemed to have eyes for something other than her husband.

"You're very correct. They seem to know how impressive they are. Keep your eyes peeled and I'm sure that we'll see one. Bald eagles are usually found here during the fall and winter, gorging on the spawning salmon. Their eyesight is phenomenal and can see a salmon a mile up. Their parenting skills really make them unique. When the baby eagles are fledging, the mother actually pushes them out of the nest and lets them drop quite a ways before rescuing them with her wings. With each attempt, the baby eagle either gains or loses more confidence until it finally spreads its own wings out of necessity and starts flying."

"What an interesting way to kick the kids out of the nest so to speak," said Sharman, wondering if the technique would have worked with her own children. They never left the nest until she did.

Sharman spread her financial wings on this trip yet saved some money by rooming with her friends. Once she returned home, her nest was closed to her young. They would have to find a place to live and learn to survive without her.

Sharman never realized how much she enjoyed being on the water with those around her. She wondered if Gerard had a nest. There was no ring, no tan indicator, so maybe he was nestless. A bit young perhaps but, oh boy, could he function under stress. He was a natural controller. Sharman respected that and wanted to know him better. Sharman was interested why he was drawn to birds instead of people.

"Maggie, look over there at six o'clock," shouted Dewey, decked out in his English best ready to be photographed himself.

It was a school of dolphins prancing in and out of the water, knowing how delightful they were. As we looked, a group of young whales with their caretakers followed knowing that they could compete with their own antics.

I was so pleased with all the sightings. The marine wildlife didn't disappoint us. Sometimes the conditions were pristine, you had your binoculars, the weather was good, the water was calm, but nothing was happening in the water. Once the negative energy started, it just kept building and nothing was seen. I was glad today wasn't one of those days, but instead filled with anticipated photographs.

The captain even contributed when he permitted some of the passengers to help steer the rig. Hours passed and it suddenly occurred to me that noon tea was out of the question. It would be more like three o'clock tea. If I were late, I hoped the professor would not be offended. He and Sara didn't sign up for the whaling excursion, nor did Ariel and Dotty. Funny, usually it was the highlight of the trip. Both of the couples had health issues but I hoped it wouldn't curtail their appetite for adventure. This was the chance of a lifetime to see whales in their natural habitat. National Geographic was one thing, but this was up close and personal.

It was early in the morning and Sara's adventure was to explore Vancouver Island by herself. She wanted to find that rocky beach and wondered how faraway it was from the hotel. Before leaving, she had grabbed a map, but she lacked a sense of direction. It was a touring map highlighting intellectual things that were offered on the island. Natural habitat was on her mind nothing else.

From Girl Scouts, Sara knew that the sun rises in the East and sets in the West, and that moss grew on the north side of the tree, but these trees were not mossy. She could read a compass but didn't have one. Half of the island was documented on the map. She wanted undocumented, no streets, and no traffic lights or stop signs. Before she plunged into the park, she took one long look back trying to get oriented.

Sara followed her instinct. The diversified park was full of flowers, and trees; big trees not the four footers down in Texas. There were lofty pines and huge chestnut trees.

New England danced in front of her eyes. What she wouldn't give to move back to Connecticut. She still couldn't believe that she had actually left. But a deal was a deal, and she promised her mother if by thirty, her modeling career was still unrealistic, she would relocate to Texas. Thirty came and went. So did she, to Texas. Her parents literally came and dragged her away, towing her little sports car, caging up her uncooperative cat, and ending her unrealized dreams.

When Sara first arrived, Texas had nothing for her, and she planned endless weekend trips back to Connecticut, hoping she might kidnap herself and never have to return. But the trip never happened and gradually she found the flat beach off the flat road down the flat highway. Mountains and seasons couldn't be replaced.

The monotonous heat and humidity in Texas was enough to drive anyone to do anything. She did. Marriage was something she had vowed never to do. Her husband was a retired professor, well-respected, well-liked, but hated everything that she loved.

After four years of dating, Sara thought she knew Leon but didn't. Did anyone really know the significant other? Most people pretended to like something that they didn't or be someone that they weren't just to please. I mean when you got down to it, no one really wanted to be alone in the good times or the bad. Sometimes just to have someone else care was enough. Sara outgrew the caring stage.

Making a spiritual sound, the wind whistled through the pines. A pine grove was comforting, whether it was covered with maiden snow or brushed by whirling winds. That rushing sound was etched in her memory.

Today, she didn't have to rely on her memory; everything was right before her. The intoxicating pines permitted her entry, and she made note of which gardens she passed and how she passed them. Straight ahead she heard some squawking noises, and there not ten feet away was a lily pond with four baby ducklings and their adoring mom.

Ducks were something else that she was partial to since the New England couple who lived across the street adopted hundreds of them without filling out any paperwork. Every morning, she fed the feathered flocks handfuls of dried corn and directed them with her mimicked honking. She could call a duck across the pond and then humiliate it when it found out she wasn't a duck.

This mother duck was so watchful with their ducklings, checking, always checking every move that they made. A part of Sara wished for a moment she could jump right in and get in line. It would just make everything so much easier. But the other part of Sara didn't need or want to be in a line. She was so thankful that there were no lines of people anywhere in sight.

For a few hours, she trudged happily along coming across the most unbelievable sight. Flashy, beautiful feathers were widely displayed. Honking loudly, it was a peacock. Sara wasn't sure what all the racket was about but this peacock wanted somebody's attention. Of course it was a female somebody.

A petting zoo was in the middle of nowhere. Baby goats, baby calves, baby birds, and baby dogs were all mixed up together. A wonderful eccentric couple, the caretakers, apparently lived right by the enclosed barbed wire and monitored the daily activities. Oddly their living quarters seemed to be part of the zoo. Animals were walking in and out of the worn-out cabin and were not curtailed.

Some people preferred animals. This couple seemed perfectly content with their isolation and cabin visitors. They had permitted me to enter even though I didn't have the dollar entry fee. It put things back into perspective, witnessing two very happy people who were living on entry fees. They were disheveled, wrinkled, and fulfilled. Tucking this tender photograph into her mind, she headed towards the coastline.

Smelling the saltwater, she noticed that the trees thinned out and the soil was sandy. Her heart held its breath. In front of her were huge rocky boulders as if someone dropped them down like pebbles.

The ocean's persistent waves lapped at their edges filling the crevices with a mixture of seaweed and snails. Drenched with contentment, Sara clamored on top of the nearest boulder and sat down. Popping seaweed, she felt the slimy kelp in between her fingers. The snails caught in the seaweed popped in and out of their protective shells. Hungry, Sara envisioned garlic-soaked escargot.

Relaxed, Sara somehow permitted Gerard to wiggle into her thoughts. At first, it annoyed her. Part of her wished that they were enjoying the slimy seaweed and salty ocean air together. Another part of her didn't and confirmed that it was a ridiculous thought. If anyone could be here, it would be Leon.

Sara stopped thinking and focused on the waves. That's when she heard it. Being in a trancelike state, the sound took her completely by surprise. Turning around, she saw a middle-aged man watching her. Sara's survival instinct swirled into readiness.

This was exactly what could happen when you went off by yourself, her mother's voice pounded in her ears. Before she left, she had promised her mother she wouldn't go off by herself. Here she was very much alone, very vulnerable, and she knew it. Would this rocky coastline be her demise? She had to do something quickly so she started coughing recklessly: loudly, obnoxiously, and almost without breathing. In any way that she could, she had to dissuade this man. Irritated and surprised, the watcher quickly disappeared as his perched target vanished. Sara was so thankful for her disgusting coughing ability. Getting off the isolated beach and finding other people was a necessity. Suddenly as if on cue, there were loud noises and a caravan of loud people appeared. Sara realized the danger. It was a close call with a creepy balding man.

The sun crossed the sky and started heading down. Sara heard Leon's concern. A road lay straight ahead and she clung to it. Mulling the incident over in her mind, Sara came to the realization that she could probably outrun any creep that tried to bother her. But she didn't want to be tested. Sara could see the headlines: Teacher Assaulted on Isolated Seashore Boulder. Her ways had to change. It was too close. His eyes were still on her. For the rest of the trip and maybe even for the rest of her life, Sara wouldn't venture off on her own again.

Leon waited for his own adventure. It was way past twelve and Leon couldn't help but worry that something might have derailed Maggie. His leg hurt.

Leon had mixed feelings about the tea venture. But if Gerard were there, the conversation would be light and airy. Personal details often lead to personal misunderstandings. Taking another pain pill, he waited for the deadening, waited for the nerves to stop their harassment.

Just then the phone rang. It was Maggie who apologized for the delay. The whales were out in force so the excursion took a little longer than expected. In thirty minutes, Leon agreed to meet her in the lobby. Leon hoped that Gerard also got the message.

When Leon approached the lobby, Gerard was nowhere in sight and his demeanor changed. Maggie's smile soothed him. Leon's guard dropped.

"Gerard was tired from the whaling excursion," exclaimed Maggie, relieved that there would just be the two of them. Then she remembered Sara. "Is Sara going to join us?" She held her breath, hoping the answer was no.

"Sara, she left hours ago. She couldn't wait to find the beach."

"The closest beach is a ways away."

"Sara loves a challenge. Regardless of the odds, when she makes up her mind to do something, she does it. Stubbornness is Sara's middle name."

Maggie got quiet. Maggie knew stubborn. It was also her middle name.

"The whales gave everyone quite a show," commented Maggie, very content knowing now it would be so much easier.

"How's your phantom pain today? Leon, does being around the water increase the pressure?"

Maggie cared. Her concern attached itself to Leon. He couldn't shake it off. It was nice to have someone worry about him instead of completely disregarding him, his aliments, the way Sara sometimes did. It wasn't really her fault since he always hurt. Daily, pain devoured him. He didn't know how much walking he could do.

"Maggie, how faraway is the Empress Hotel?"

"Oh, don't worry. I have a cab waiting out front to take us down." Leon smiled inside. He appreciated her organizing the outing. He decided to sit back and let Maggie take control. She personified a tour director on and off duty. Leon liked women who were in control and could make their own decisions. Something that Sara had trouble with.

The cab ride was quick. The immense Empress Hotel shouted out its grandeur. The harbor mirrored the chalet's charm. Staring, Leon envisioned snow-crested mountains surrounding it.

"You see the snow-covered mountains don't you? Remember, this is English architecture, a combination of castles and chalets. It was built at the turn of the century," piped Maggie, wanting to impress the professor with anything she knew. Leon was transfixed as he entered the flower-embossed gardens, which lead up to the entrance of the hotel. The elegance drowned his pain. Then he saw the stairs.

"Maggie, I need to take the stairs slowly. Maggie didn't miss a beat. She wrapped one arm carefully around Leon's waist and carefully guided him up the stairs. It was natural for her. Maggie knew the care that Leon needed. Leon watched Maggie's face for any reluctance, but there wasn't any. There was only assurance. Leon wished now that Sara were here so that she could see how easy it was to help him. Sara resented helping Leon so he stopped asking.

Before Leon knew it, they were seated in the starched, gilded-columned, opulent dining room sipping from china-inlaid cups and munching on tasty tidbits. Leon inhaled the calories as Maggie cast her spell.

"Now wasn't this worth the effort?" chimed Maggie, making sure Leon had everything within his reach. "I always try to visit here at least for tea. The meal menus are a bit pricey for just one person so I enjoy the beauty in a more affordable way."

Leon knew Maggie had a thrifty side. He could tell by the way she dressed so unlike Sara who had to have the best, especially when she traveled.

Maggie's cavalier attitude toward life explained her casualness. It was refreshing. Maggie was the type of woman who told it like it was, and if you didn't like what she said, it didn't seem to bother her a bit. Personally, Leon thought Gerard and Maggie would have a lot in common. Too bad he wasn't here.

Leon didn't expect to enjoy Maggie's company as much as he did. In sudden unison, both reached for the very same crumpet. Fingers touched unexpectedly. It was purely random. They halved it. Leon's professor side gave in. He relaxed. All defenses halted. Maggie was so easy to talk with. She shared her strengths and her concerns. Curiously, some of her concerns were about Leon.

"Leon, why did you decide to go on a bus tour when you can hardly walk?" Maggie asked with a twinkle in her eye. Leon thought maybe it was a trick question because there wasn't really a sensible answer. But he shared in spite of himself.

"It was an anniversary present for Sara and me, mostly Sara who loves anything with mountains and trees. I just happened to be part of the package. To be honest with you, I didn't think there would be so many frequent stops. I suppose it's a good idea for most people but not for the handicapped. Everyday just reaffirms to me just how handicapped I actually am. An illuminated sticker is always on my forehead. It's too bad that people notice my inabilities first."

"Don't you think it's possible that people may be drawn to you because of your inabilities?"

"No, you couldn't convince me of that by the way they almost ran me over when getting off the bus. But I wised up and now just sit and wait for the stampede to empty."

"But what about Gus, Gerard, and the others who stayed back with you and made sure that you got off safely?"

"You're right; some do care but—"

"No, Leon, many care and are always asking me what they can do to help you. In fact, there's a faith healer on the bus. Tomorrow she's going to sit with you and try to take some of your pain away."

"Really, how surprising. I'm certain Sara isn't going to like that."

"But it's about you, not Sara, am I right?"

"Regardless, Sara would never permit another woman to take her designated spot on the bus. But it's a nice gesture just the same. Thank the faith healer for her concern. Was the lady from Israel? I met her and knew she was caring, the way she shook my hand."

"Yes, that's the one. She's here with her husband to celebrate her remission."

"Her remission?"

"Her cancer remission. She was diagnosed with full-blown liver cancer and somehow beat it back. But I'll let her tell you the rest. I don't want to divulge anything that might affect her healing ability."

I gazed at the professor longingly for a split second only wanting to help him then quickly pulled myself away from his gaze. The ambiance of the room was easily distracting. I needed to get redirected.

"Remember it's my treat," I reminded Leon as he instinctively picked up the bill.

"Maggie, are you sure? I mean I didn't realize it would be so expensive."

"With my discount, it's nothing really."

Usually when the professor felt overcharged, he made a point to challenge it. He didn't have to. Maggie paid the bill and they were off to the Parliament building across the street.

Parliament was a regal type of government. Crowds of people were lounging in the huge yards topped with marble statues and spouting water fountains. Frisbees were being thrown and tourists were going this way and that. Some directed, some not. It reminded Leon of the collegiate atmosphere, its relaxed structure, especially when the students took time to enjoy themselves in between classes.

In a moment, everything changed. A raging alarm suddenly pierced the laughter. It was a lock down. People raced away from the Parliament building as guards surfaced like ants and randomly checked unsuspecting passports.

"Leon, this is not the day for a tour as you might guess there has been a security breach and when this happens, Canadians don't treat it lightly. We need to leave, but not too quickly as guards had cordoned off the area.

"Maggie, I don't have my passport."

"Don't worry, I have mine, and you're with me."

Leon just couldn't believe what he saw and heard. It was as if all sanity had been questioned. Tourists were being lined up and checked. Leon suddenly remembered that he was not in the United States and felt the vulnerability of being a foreigner. Sara would never believe this. He was thankful that she wasn't here. With her nervous demeanor, they would have checked her right away. Maggie quickly edged toward the street wasting little time. In one instant, they were vulnerable, in the next, just thankful tourists.

"Leon, it happens. The Parliament building is so accessible that once in a while individuals take advantage of it."

Leon was glad to be with a seasoned Canadian who knew what could happen on and off the streets. He never wanted to feel that anxiety again, making a mental note to always carry his passport.

"Maggie, that just physically wiped me out. I better head back to the hotel where I can relax safely."

I couldn't believe it—of all the days for Canadians to misbehave themselves. Leon would have loved the Parliament building noting his interest in history and government, maybe another time. But when I looked at Leon's drained face, I knew there wouldn't be another time. Leon leaned against a railing and I knew he needed to get back to the hotel.

Just up ahead, there was a waiting taxicab ready to be of service. The outing was such a nice diversion for me. I wondered if Leon had felt anything but pain since we left the hotel. My growing attraction towards the professor needed to be nurtured carefully, quietly.

Sara was in trouble. She couldn't find her way back to the hotel. All her careful observations had backfired. She didn't remember where to turn and the pine trees eluded her. Somehow she had gotten offtrack and desperately needed some divine intervention. As she plodded along, she wished now that she had stayed with Leon or had gone on a scholastic outing with Dotty and Ariel. Then she found herself on the other side of the park not at the entrance, but on the north side since there was a bit of moss growing on a pine tree closest to her. Everything was turned around. She had to find some road that took her back to the hotel. Looking up, she remembered the ornate tops of the buildings. That was her compass.

Her elegant hotel rooftop was fringed with gold leaf and dipped in a shade of light green. Another hour passed. There was the etched roof and its splendor. Sara was never so happy to see a roofline in all her life.

POSSIBILITIES

||||||||||||||||||||||||||||||||||||||||||||||||||||||||||||||||||||||||||||||||||||||||||||||||||||||||||||||||||||||||||

S ara had quite enough of self adventure and couldn't wait to spend
some time with Dotty and Ariel, especially over a plate of pasta.
Exhausted, Leon rested from his afternoon thriller. Sara couldn't
believe that a tea date almost ended up in being arrested. Anything was
possible; they were tourists.

Sara was relieved that Maggie invited Leon out and couldn't wait
to thank her. Leon's disability prevented him from joining the various
side trips. Guards and all, Sara was happy that he visited the Parliament
building.

Famished, Sara only thought of food and met Ariel and Dotty outside
in front of the hotel. Unexpectedly, there was another hungry face, Gerard.
Sara had mixed feelings at seeing him. Her ocean daydream rushed back
to her, flooding her senses with concern. Right in front of her, Gerard
winked. He knew.

Dotty and Ariel were a pair of reporters. They critiqued their outing,
going to a huge cinema with a six-story-high screen viewing historical-and-
nature-based movies.

Sara decided to leak her own news story.

"So you haven't heard about Maggie and Leon almost getting arrested?"
All eyes and ears were on Sara.

"Well, what became of it? I mean how much safer could Leon have
been than with Maggie." questioned Gerard, wishing now he had gone
just for the experience.

The smell of sausage, sauce, and cheese wafted down the street. They
reached their destination and couldn't sit down quickly enough. Ordering
their food, they basked in the smells.

Sara was certain Gerard sat next to her just to test her concentration level.

"Thirsty?" Gerard asked Sara.

Sara diligently searched for the lone olive at the bottom of her margarita. Gerard watched Sara devour her olive aware of the effects that olives have on some women. He hoped that Sara might become more aware of him.

Not indulging in alcohol frequently, Sara forgot about its numbing effects. Somehow she tipped her glass and it spilled into Gerard's lap.

"What did I do?" Sara grabbed a handful of napkins quickly soaking up the spilled margarita. Shocked, Ariel and Dotty quickly looked the other way. Gerard just smiled broadly enjoying Sara's flushed, embarrassed face.

"Would you care for another olive-ladened margarita or maybe a Cognac?"

There was that gentleness, that caring. Sara wasn't use to gentleness. She was usually the one who fixed things and always felt the need to solve any dilemma that showed its confused face.

Sara had two legs and was expected to function regardless of why or what. Her nerve endings were trained for trauma. Gerard's easy grin numbed her. Sara felt a new sense of freedom.

Tonight, no one expected anything from her except to enjoy herself so she did. She actually listened to the conversation. Sara didn't recognize who she became. Without her permission, things changed. Here, there wasn't any pain. She didn't miss it for a second. The more Gerard talked, the more Sara wanted to know what was important to him. Inhaling their food didn't interrupt the conversation.

"What about that chiropractor of yours, how did you meet her?" asked Sara, remembering how Leon told her that Gerard had a personal masseuse.

Gerard wanted to share the surprising details of why his fiancée, Gwena, wasn't with him. Dotty and Ariel shuffled in their seats. Sara knew it wasn't exactly an appropriate question but she didn't care.

"Too many patients and Gwena didn't feel she could take the time off without letting someone down. When a back goes out, as you well know, there's nothing quite like that pain and anyone does anything to get rid of it."

"You mean pay anything to get rid of it, right?" Sara replied knowing the pain. "Chiropractors can pretty much charge anything for any procedure. It seems completely unregulated as far as charges go. Am I right about that? I know with my chiropractor if he pushed for five minutes or fifteen, it's still the same charge. Well, I guess pain takes precedence——I know mine did. When you're hurting, you just don't care. But I wonder if chiropractors ever get questioned about their procedures and their costs?"

"Gwena doesn't overcharge. Chiropractors regulate themselves through their association. Word would get around if a chiropractor persistently took advantage over his or her patients. It's just like any doctor. Doctor's fees are just what they are. They're usually high, but often one doesn't have a choice. But right now, we do have a choice so what will be our after-dinner entertainment?"

They could hear strumming guitars from the next room. Before Sara knew it, they were ushered into a room filled with swirling couples swaying effortlessly to the music. An elderly violinist played the right rhythm but was off in a few notes. It didn't seem to matter to anyone. That was the beauty of it. No one cared, least of all the violinist.

Since Sara played the violin, she wanted to jump up and take over, but Gerard had other plans for her. Much to her surprise, Gerard pulled her toward the dance floor. At first Gerard kept a good amount of distance between them then pulled her closer as if an afterthought. Sara had never been twirled or dipped as much as in those short twenty minutes. Gerard made up for all those danceless nights in her past. He was in command.

Gerard had Sara just where he wanted her. She seemed interested. He gave her his complete undivided attention. Gerard sensed that something was missing in Sara's life. Maybe he could help her realize what it was. Maybe destiny intervened. Gerard wasn't sure. He was sure that he wasn't going to relinquish these feelings until he unearthed them. Gerard reached for Sara's hand. Sara quickly pulled her hand back. In a second, Gerard's control vanished. For Sara, it was only about the music, the dancing. She hoped his red face would understand and regain its composure.

As Sara looked around, there were a few other red faces, exhausted faces. Dotty and Ariel were ready to leave so the tired couple reminded younger ears about the arduous day ahead of them at the Butchart Gardens. Prompting was not necessary and before they knew it Ariel had spotted that medical supply store near the hotel, and purchased a cushy pair of crutches for Leon and safely stowed them under his determined arms. Ariel remembered Leon told him his were shot. Within minutes, they were back at the hotel lobby and spied Maggie's nose deep in paperwork.

Maggie looked up in horror at the clutched crutches.

"What happened, Ariel? Have Dotty's knees finally given up?"

So far everyone moved fairly well except maybe the professor who was exhausted. No answer was needed.

"Sara, is Leon going to be able to go with the group to the gardens tomorrow?" Now, I needed an answer.

"Hopefully Leon will walk better with these."

Sara's words worried me since tomorrow was only about walking through the paths of gorgeous flowers, bushes, and budding trees that resided in the well-preserved garden sanctuary.

I needed to call ahead and make sure that they had a wheelchair, so that Sara could push him through some of the sculptured gardens. Even a pair of sturdy crutches would not give the professor the mobility that he needed. I wasn't certain if they even had wheelchairs.

As tour directors, we were always ready for exceptions, ready for the unexpected. Sara seemed fairly relaxed. Perhaps things were not as bad as they appeared. I couldn't help but visualize Leon, hopping around up in his suite, needing help that wasn't there. Tomorrow I was determined to help Leon with or without Sara's permission and I did.

THE GARDEN'S CHAIR

||||||||||||||||||||||||||||||||||||||||||||||||||||||||||||||||||||||||||||||||||||||||||||||||||||||||||||||||||||||||||||||||

With Gus' extra effort, we were off. Everyone was accounted for even the professor who moved slowly, sporting his new crutches. There were many concerned looks but his wasn't one of them. For Leon, staying behind wasn't an option. I wanted to surprise Leon about the wheelchair. It was ready and waiting for him.

Gus started singing "On the Road Again," and spirits were in high gear. It is amazing how much difference a few days off the bus made. Two days ago, monotonous bus mileage was etched in many of the tourists' faces. Today you would never have known it. It was as though it were the first day on the bus. There was nothing like free days spent eating, buying, and exploring interesting shops. With binoculars in hand, they were now ready for the awaiting gardens. Gus toned down the singing. That was my cue.

"The Butchart Gardens were thirteen miles from Victoria and covered a sprawling fifty-five acres. It was originally a worn-out limestone quarry that supplied Mr. Butchart's cement business. During their worldwide travels, the Butchart's collected rare and exotic plants, trees, and flowers, creating their famous sunken garden. There was also a Japanese, Italian, and Rose Garden.

"By 1920, more than fifty thousand visitors had seen the horticultural delight. In 2004, the gardens were a hundred years old and were designated a National Historic Site for Canada. Over a million people a year visit the sprawling gardens. We will first visit the Sunken Gardens where you can see ivy and Virginia creeper. There is a tall kiln stack, which is all that is left of the cement factory. A lake lined with Japanese maples and St. John's Wort will lead us to the Ross Fountain.

1964, Ian Ross, a grandson of the Butchart, created the fountain which spews water seventy feet high and is lit up at night. Near the fountain, there are two totem poles which commemorate the garden's one hundredth year anniversary. During the summer nights, fireworks can be viewed from the sunken garden."

There was a long disgruntled sigh on the bus.

"Sorry we won't be here tonight. Most of us will be in Chinatown lightening good luck lantern water boats."

The sigh stopped. You just needed visualizations to keep them content. I was fairly good at it and always was at least a few activities ahead of them.

"After the fountain, we'll head towards the Rose Garden."

All Sara could think about was Elizabeth Park back in Connecticut where the family visited each year when her ninety-year-old grandmother made her yearly visit. The park sported roses dressed in skirts of multi-pink, yellow, and white as well as muted colors. One of her favorites was a deep purple, almost black rose.

Once a year, contenders were judged, winners planted and numerous ribbons and awards were presented. People who grew roses tended to be very serious about their offspring, treating them like children. It was always a must for her grandmother who grew her own roses in parched Texas.

Sara heard Maggie's voice continue. "Rose-covered arches will welcome you to the frog fountain and Italian- wrought iron wishing well. Along the flagstone walk, you'll see winning hybrid tea roses labeled with their country of origin. Hiding among the roses you'll find a pair of bronze sturgeons from Florence, Italy, guarding the Sturgeon Fountain.

"There are many fountains in the gardens highlighting the different landscapes and floral patterns. A winding stream leads you to the Japanese gardens one of my favorites. Rare Himalayan blue poppies line the garden. This garden was started with the help of a Japanese landscaper in 1906. If you look closely, you can see the ocean from this site and your ears might hear the roar of seaplanes which land near the dock in Butchart cove. Also, look for moored international boats.

"Star Pond is just beyond the Japanese gardens, where Mr. Butchart introduced his collection of ornamental ducks. Most eyes were still focused on me, so I continued not wanting to leave anything out. Their evaluations always appreciated the intimate tidbits; at least that was what they indicated. There's a bronze statue of Mercury between two arched entrances that leads to the Italian Garden where you'll see a cross-shaped pond fed by a fountain, a girl holding a fish. It's hard to imagine that this area was once a concrete-floored tennis court."

Right now, Sara's mind needed a rest from the continued conversation. How many gardens were there? She could never be a tour director. Maggie was a natural and looked like she was enjoying sharing every single detail.

The more she shared, the more Sara wondered how in the world Leon was going to hop through each and every garden. Would he even be able to hop through one? The reality of the situation dawned on Sara because she knew she would have to stay with him and miss all the beauty. She resented the entire situation and wished for once that she could just enjoy something without worrying about everything.

Maggie continued, "You may get hungry by this time and you can purchase refreshments at the piazza, which is right after the Italian gardens. While you're munching and purchasing various items at the seed and gift shop, you'll see the former Butchart residence and a Florentine bronze statue of Tacca the boar. Last but not least are the Mediterranean gardens where you'll find drought-resistant plants from all over the world.

"After that you'll find a beige tour bus ready to take you back to the hotel."

A roaring cheer went up and someone commented that they felt they had already taken the tour. Hopefully it was just a bit of pent-up bus humor.

It was quite steep as the bus slowly climbed higher and higher towards its destination. Many tour buses were on the road making passing a lesson in strategy. Gus was good at it, but I wished he would slow down. It was rocky as well and one false move would get us stuck ruining our good timing. I assured, our guide, Ms. Montaine that we would be there by 10:00 a.m. so that we joined the other race horses at the starting gate. Ms. Montaine brought the headphones and usually narrated as we strolled along. Talk about an earful.

Every flower, every country was mentioned. The guests loved the dialogue, especially the flower enthusiasts. At the end of the tour, any seed from any flower could be purchased in the seed shop which was an unexpected novelty.

Much to my relief, Gus slowed down. Maybe it was that last cup of coffee he gulped down earlier. He gave me an assured look although his calmness changed quickly as he got to the parking lot. A few cars had parked illegally, giving him quite a distance between two vehicles making sure that the bus had enough room to pass. Gus always did things in a nonchalant way as not to worry the tourists, but if I saw him measuring the distance so did others. With a grin on his face, he cracked a joke about the important of an inch and that was that.

The entranceway was pretty grand, lots of people, and lots of colorful flags from different countries. After all, their visitors were from all over the world, so it was very welcoming or maybe it was for the flowers' origins.

The chair's metal gleamed in the sun. It was an eye- catcher. Leon and Sara had no idea that the chair was for them and couldn't believe that I arranged it. But one look at Leon made it all worthwhile, complete relief flooded his face and his whole body relaxed.

Sara's face told quite a different story. Sara already decided to stay with Leon for a little while then go off exploring with the rest of the group. Now everything changed. How in the world was Sara going to push Leon without pulling her back out? His 225-pound frame was now even a little bit heavier after all the vacation goodies. Afterwards, she would need a pair of crutches as well. Her face tightened.

"Sara, don't worry, I can wheel myself around the paths. It should be a lot quicker this way. Just wait and see."

The rest of the group had already arrived at the Sunken Gardens and that's when Sara turned off her headset. She didn't want to hear about what she couldn't see. Leon's plan might have worked if the path hadn't been uphill all the way.

Once the group was in another's hands, Maggie usually went her own way. It gave her time to relax and think about the next day's events. As she strolled along, she couldn't help but notice the professor and his struggling wife. Sara was no match for these hills but she was, being stronger and used to pushing chairs since her father was confined to one.

"Sara, can I help you? I'm twice your size and will be able to get Leon up those hills." Without warning, Sara's chair sentence abruptly ended. Maggie offered and with no hesitation, Sara accepted. A tremendous weight was lifted off of her. Her dreading turned into enjoyment.

"Go on, Sara, Maggie and I will be fine."

Leon was relieved as well since all he could hear was Sara sighing in between puffing. Maggie didn't puff and didn't sigh. While she pushed him, she actually talked to him. What a welcome relief. Now he didn't have to worry about taking the beauty away from Sara. Sara hurried down the path and disappeared. She couldn't wait to catch up with the others.

I was finally alone with the professor.

"Leon, tell me about being a professor. What did you enjoy about it the most? Do you think you'll ever go back to teaching even part time?"

Now that Maggie had Leon all to herself, she was going to ask those questions that she wanted to ask. After all, Sara left. No one asked her to leave.

"With all my health problems, I doubt it. Things are never really the same after a complicated bypass surgery. The students would know. They can sense anything that's different about you. The energy level just wouldn't be there. There would be things that I couldn't do. It would affect my teaching, my delivery. I don't really have any desire to go back. Too many politics. The powers to be seem to be more interested in what you publish than what you teach. Publishing takes time that you don't normally have and since I used to work straight through the summers, I never really had that "free" time that other professors may have had. I was in love with teaching not notoriety. There really is nothing like seeing a needy disadvantaged student grasp a concept like how to write a term paper. Many of my students didn't have the writing skills that were necessary to achieve success at the college level."

I carefully phrased my next comment. "You mentioned disadvantaged students. Were they from different cultures?"

"They were mostly from the Mexican culture. They were like my own kids. I got attached to them. They didn't know how needy they were. Poverty clung to them. I helped them catch up. We all did, especially the other Mexican professors, which I could count on one hand. The college didn't discriminate; it just didn't hire Mexican professors. So there weren't many role models for the kids. I tried to make it up to them. I wanted to reach as many as I could. It was all about giving back to the students trying to close that gnawing gap."

"I bet your students adored you. You probably left quite a void when you did leave."

"I don't know. Once I left that was the end of it. After I packed my boxes and locked my office door for the last time, I had no further contact with anyone. I gave the college everything I had. It almost killed me. When I retired, I just didn't have anything left to give."

"It was Sara's turn to get whatever I had left, which wasn't very much. It took me quite a long time to recover any kind of strength after my heart operation. Then I went through that draining depression. Frankly, I'm surprised that Sara didn't leave me. She should've. I would've understood completely."

"How long did it take you to recover from your depression?"

"I never really have. With pain, you suffer."

Maggie empathized. "Most people don't understand when you're in pain, regardless of the reason. People get uneasy when they know that you're hurting. Conversation is labored, making things worse. For others, it isn't comfortable talking about what they haven't experienced."

"Maggie, when your husband left, he really traumatized you, didn't he? Earlier in the trip, I remember when you briefly told me about it."

"Certain things about certain people remind me of him. In the beginning, he had such good qualities, but time cheapened them. When he lost his job, he gave up and stopped caring about me and the children. He didn't want to be bothered by anyone or anything. Not good at being both parents, the kids could see right through me. Only his physical body was there. Then without one word of explanation, his body left. That's what unglued me. It was as if he vanished from the continent. Later on, I learned that he did just that and ended up in Mexico with a senorita."

"Maggie, maybe there wasn't an explanation. At the time maybe all he could do was disappear, to lose himself in another life since he couldn't cope with his own. I know how he felt. I was there for three years and couldn't talk to Sara or anyone else about it. My life was insignificant and all I wanted to do was end it. The only thing that prevented me was that Sara would never have been able to deal with the aftermath. Maybe your ex-husband just wanted to spare you the trauma. You know that flight-or-fight syndrome. Men don't like explanations. They don't like looking inside. Their emotions are disturbing."

"I never really thought about it in that way. It makes sense, but I certainly don't respect him for what he did to us. Maybe there was a way out for him. I wanted him to seek professional help, but he cringed at the suggestion. It was never brought up again."

"That's where he and I differed. I knew that I needed help and sought it out. That was my saving grace. It was either professional help or Sara's mock counseling. Maybe that's why I did it just to keep Sara quiet. I didn't want her to know how I was feeling, but someone had to know—I knew that much."

It was just so easy to open up to the professor and relate to him. If given the chance, I would have pushed that chair to eternity.

Sara caught up with the others and noticed some surprised looks.

"Look at her arms, she couldn't possibly push that chair," commented Gerard, secretly delighted that Sara was once again back in the group.

Ariel was concerned about Leon and couldn't understand how Sara would just leave him like that. Dotty didn't seem at all surprised, keenly aware of Sara's restless nature. Sara breathed in the beauty gulping it down. It reminded her of the flower-filled fields back in Connecticut. She was home again.

"Sara, look over there."

Gerard passed her his binoculars and she glanced at the radiant petals. It was so unusual to have someone hand her binoculars. Usually she did the handing. Gerard lost himself in nature the way that Sara did. He didn't want her to miss anything. There were so many facets to Gerard. Maybe she had overlooked some.

Gerard thought he could get Sara alone, away from the others, but he had another thought coming. Whether he picked up the pace or slowed it down, the four of them were inseparable. Gerard knew that Ariel and Dotty had Leon's best interests at heart but so did he.

"Sara, tell me about your music. It was the violin, am I right?"

"You remembered. Well, I was on a Student Council Christmas Outing warming up the kids for their performance when the violinist handed me his violin momentarily and his bow produced these magical sounds. I was spellbound.

"The next day I went down to the nearest music store to rent a violin. I started learning how to play it from the student council students who came in for weekly meetings after school. The hardest part was the bowing. It wasn't natural for me. Then one of the kids told me it was like brushing your teeth, so I finally got the right movement."

"Did you ever take real lessons?"

"No, I just bought the different book levels for the violin and taught myself. My grandfather played the violin so I guess it was genetic. Finally I mastered the vibrato, which was also an unnatural movement for me. There's nothing very natural about the violin from your twisted neck to your vibrating fingers. Practice makes sore callous fingers. But when you love it, none of it matters."

"And the piano was that by accident as well?"

"In a way I guess it was. I used to love to go to ballet classes and thought the toe shoes were the magic. But it was the piano music. Once I figured that out, I started playing and never stopped. But I can only play for me, which irritates my mother to no end. She has begged me to play for her but when someone is listening my concentration level is gone.

"It reminds me of a time when I went to a friend's piano recital, which was held in this huge auditorium. The pianist wore her finest gown, but when she sat down to play not one sound came out of that piano. Her fingers froze. Finally her music teacher had to sit beside her and turn the pages of the score which of course was supposed to be memorized. Needless to say after four grueling years of music school, she never became a concert pianist.

"Pressure does the opposite to me," Gerard volunteered. "The more pressure I have, the more I excel. People expect a lot from me, but I expect tons more from myself. When we have deadlines at work, I mentally push the deadlines up even sooner so I expect those around me to put in twice the work because I naturally do. I have a lot of younger men and women who work for me and they privately renamed me Grandpa. I guess it was their way of getting back in an acceptable manner. They can call me anything they want as long as the work gets done."

Sara could just see Gerard ordering the kids around. Compared to those twenty-five year olds he might look a bit like grandpa. Sara was sure that at school her seventh graders had some delightful nicknames for her as well.

"At school, we have expected deadlines. Every three weeks, our grades are due and that never changes. Mentally, I push myself with the papers, correcting them on time. Teaching in and of itself is rewarding, but it's getting corrected papers passed back that wears you down literally, especially the honors' classes. They have project deadlines, but so do you since you have to read the turned-in projects, compare them, and then give them a grade that they're sure to question.

"The parents put so much pressure on them to make the A. I'm never surprised when I hear about an honor student who just plain fizzled out by his senior year when his grades really counted. My parents wanted me to try in school, but they didn't demand that I make all As. Some of these kids already have migraines at the age of twelve."

"School has changed," Gerard noted. "Many parents want Ivy League and nothing else will do. I know. I'm the product of one such union. It was Harvard or nothing. So it became Harvard. It was a game for me because I already knew that I was smart enough to make it and did. The acceptance letter just meant playing the real game and that's how I viewed it. I studied hard, but put just as much energy into making friends who're still my friends to this day.

"College was about making contacts and that's part of the reason why I'm where I am now. You never know when an influential friend can help you out. Once in a while, you get yourself into situations that you can't solve by yourself."

Sara felt a bit guilty leaving Leon so abruptly. She was thankful that the others couldn't see it. Gardens came and went. Before Sara and the others knew it, they were handling exotic seeds. To her surprise, Maggie and Leon were already at the seed shop enjoying a glass of ice-cold lemonade and a vegetarian sandwich with leafy greens.

"How did you get here before us?" asked Sara, relieved to see Leon's face dancing with smiles. She examined it for any undertones. There weren't any. Maggie's face was dancing as well. Maybe it was the sandwich. Sara quickly ordered one and sat down.

"Sara, did you get to go through all the gardens?" asked Leon, casually noting that his wife seemed anxious and couldn't understand why. She had done just what she wanted to do and should be ecstatic. She wasn't. Then he realized it had to be the time element. "Sara, we didn't go that far before we both got tired." That seemed to set her off even more. Sara wondered how long they had been munching on their greens.

Leon had enjoyed himself more than he expected, and Sara would just have to readjust.

Watching Leon eat rabbit food in the seed store was one thing but this was quite another. Maggie went ahead of the others to get Leon settled on the bus and return the worn-out wheelchair to its rightful owner.

Gus herded everyone on the bus. Sara waited until the line dwindled. She didn't care for being bunched up in between people. In fact she hated it. Once on the bus, she noticed that her seat beside Leon was taken. Not with some older frail woman, but a young vibrant women who was smiling and laughing with her husband. Sara paused beside her seat but nothing happened. The seat snatcher just smiled at her and the determined lady behind her just wanted to get by. With little choice, Sara kept walking down the bus aisle looking for somewhere to sit. All eyes were fastened to her like buttons on a sweater. Their questioning stares screamed of confusion. Sara hated being the center of attention. Finally she saw a single seat at the very back of the bus. As she sat down, Sara couldn't keep her disbelieving eyes off the seat snatcher. The lady's hand was massaging Leon's right leg, up and down in a circular motion. Feeling violently ill inside, Sara started to rise up when she felt a reassuring hand on her shoulder urging her back down.

"My wife is a faith healer. She wants to help your hurting husband." Sara's puffed-up face deflated like a popped tire. As Sara looked closer, she could see the lady praying with Leon.

"I didn't know. No one told me. I didn't know what to think."

"I told my wife it was a bad idea but she insisted. You know how determined women can be." Sara saw Leon's oversized crutches sticking out of the seat.

Studying the concerned man, Sara recognized him as the husband who chatted with Leon in the seed shop. In a stupor, Sara shrunk back into her seat. She felt so ridiculous, so foolish. Without another word, the alerted husband returned to his seat.

The bus was quieter than usual. When I turned around, Lydia, the Israeli faith healer, prayed with Leon. Earlier, Lydia asked if she could change seats with Sara for awhile. I didn't see any reason why she couldn't.

Sara, I assumed, would find another seat and be happy with a little extra room. I misjudged the situation.

Sara wanted to disappear along with the others. Quietly, I got up to calm some rattled nerves. Maybe this was not quite the place or time for the intervention. No one really seemed to know what was going on. When Lydia prayed, the looks softened and everyone relaxed except Sara. Concerned, I couldn't get to Sara quickly enough.

"Sara, I guess you got bumped from your seat. But here in the back you have a chance to see so much more. Lydia is a faith healer and just wanted to relieve Leon of some of his phantom pain. Anything's worth a try, right?" Sara looked at me as if listening to the radio; a completely blank stare covered her face. Sara really didn't need another explanation. It just meant more attention. She just wanted to be left alone.

"I'm fine. I was just uneasy." Sara was convincing. Maggie left. Sara's mind raced. Not wanting everyone on the bus to feel sorry for her, Sara moved right next to Gerard. There now they would really have something to talk about.

Sara must be a mind reader. The whole trip Gerard wanted Sara to sit next to him and she did. Leon was preoccupied. It was up to Gerard to calm Sara down. He knew all about Lydia and her husband and couldn't wait to tell Sara. Gerard made it his business to know.

Gerard wished he could pull Sara closely to him and reassure her. Gerard thought better of it when he realized that he was within striking range of Leon's crutches. Leon liked Gerard but he liked his wife more.

"Lydia has been through a critical bout of cancer. She was diagnosed with the deadly disease and chemotherapy failed. She refused to die and started training for her life with a faith healer. The cancer is no longer in her body. The doctors said that it was impossible to be cured. It wasn't.

"This trip is a testimony to their faith. Her husband supported her, and also got involved with the healing ministry. Since being cured, Lydia has evolved into a faith healer herself and tries to help as many people as she can."

Sara felt so overwhelmed, so thankful, so out of place. Sara couldn't wait to get back to her original seat. Grateful, Sara would make it up to Lydia anyway that she could.

Ariel and Dotty sat right in front of Sara and couldn't help but overhear parts of the conversation. They wanted to give Sara time to regain composure before they added their supportive comments. Lydia stopped praying, and the whole bus breathed a deep sigh of relief. The forty others were especially quiet not wanting to interfere with the healing process. The chatter started.

Gerard was well aware that his daydream was over before he had time to enjoy any of it. As if nothing had happened, Lydia got up, returned to her seat beside her concerned husband, closed her eyes, and didn't utter a single word to anyone. Before the whispering started, Sara was back beside her relaxed husband.

"Sara, Lydia really helped and calmed me. My pain is gone and hopefully won't return. Her praying was very powerful. I never experienced such strong outward faith from a stranger. It's spontaneous, it just happened. It's probably more of a shock to me than to you." Leon smiled. That made up for all the prying looks. Maybe now Leon could enjoy what was left of the trip and go with her to the Chinese extravaganza later this evening.

Sara waited with Leon so that the others could scurry off the bus. All Sara wanted to do was to thank Lydia for her selflessness and her shared faith. But by the time they got off, there was no one in sight. Leon couldn't wait to get up to their room. The last thirty minutes were very intense. He was exhausted and needed to lie down.

"Sara, help me out here before I collapse." *So much for Chinese lanterns,* thought Sara, another romantic night alone. She could hardly wait to get back on that bus by herself.

CHINESE LANTERNS

I wondered how many diners would make it to Chinatown tonight. There were some tired faces. Fifteen couples made reservations. Little groups formed here and there. On any trip, it was so great when individuals bonded together. Often clients e-mailed me about continued friendships that evolved long after the trip.

I wondered if there is a chance of a friendship with Leon after he handed me my evaluation envelope. I hoped so. Sara liked me, but I hoped Leon liked me more. Sara boarded the bus right on time without her significant other. In fact, she was the only representative of the group. Then I remembered that Dotty and Ariel had plenty of Chinese food in California, and Gerard wanted to explore the nightlife by himself.

It was my perfect chance to reconnect with Sara. Changing, my outfit was very authentic, very appropriate for the evening. It amazed me how the tourists were always so aware of what I wore and when I wore it. Maybe it was a compliment in that they had absolutely nothing else to be concerned about. At night, everyone looked and acted differently, ready for possibilities. For evening events, I allowed everyone to sit where they felt comfortable. Purposely Sara moved her seat closer to mine. It was exactly what I wanted.

"It's a different crowd tonight, Sara. I'll need a little help directing traffic once we get off the bus. Are you interested?"

Sara was glad for the invite. The sooner she got involved with something other than her thoughts the better. The odor of Gus' cologne swirled up my nose. He put enough on to douse a Chinese fire. Especially at night, Gus always thought there was a chance for us. The smell triggered my awaiting comments.

"First, we'll visit a Chinese apothecary where you'll see various medicines blended, ground, and packaged. You may purchase any medicine that you like or maybe some Chinese herbs for cooking. Once we get to the store, Mr. Wang will be happy to assist you. The outside of the store doesn't look like much but the inside is a treasure trove of Chinese rituals. Mr. Wang will explain what the various medicines are used for and how to administer them."

"Does he have any headache remedies?" asked one of the Australian widowers who was pale and not feeling well. I just hoped she didn't get sick in the restaurant where the seating was so close together and there was no airflow. Hopefully Mr. Wang could help.

"Before dinner, there'll be a short lesson in using chopsticks." I don't know why, but Chinese food always tasted better when eaten with chopsticks. "The movement is really quite simple," and I demonstrated it with a traveling pair just for the occasion. "If you prefer to use forks and knives go ahead. It'll be an authentic Chinese dinner, with the Chinese kimonos, lyrical music, and waitresses darting in and out like fireflies."

It had been a while since Sara enjoyed Chinese cuisine. Chinese women were so tiny, so fragile, and so perfect with their quiet little feet and shuffling movements. She loved the singsong rhythm of their speech.

"After dinner, we'll go on a walking tour where you'll get to see the storefronts and some of the residential housing. The grand finale will be when we release little boat lanterns and make good wishes."

"Maggie, we're here," Gus softly interrupted me, looking like he already made his wish.

"Sara, there isn't a lot of room in the apothecary. If you can route the people single file into the store, that'll be helpful. We don't want to trample Mr. Wang."

Just like school. Sara was the first person off the bus. If she hadn't known there was an apothecary at that exact spot, she would have missed it. She herded the others into the small cramped store with a door big enough for only one person at a time to enter. With a ceremonial bow, the gracious Mr. Wang greeted. This intriguing Chinese gentleman fascinated Sara with his calming presence that permeated everything around him.

Speaking in soft broken English phrases, Mr. Wang shuffled down the tiny aisle, opening carefully labeled containers and scoped out handfuls of various herbs. The air filled with their fragrance. Mr. Wang proceeded to grind the herbs with a mortar and bowl as he carefully explained what herbs could be mixed together. Sara was thrilled when he allowed her to mix a concoction of herbs for the headache remedy. Waiting impatiently, the cooks in the group couldn't wait to scoop up some of the authentic herbs. Sara listened as Mr. Wang explained about the potency of cooking herbs and how to prepare Chinese recipes.

"Sara, aren't you going to purchase any culinary herbs?" I asked, noticing her lack of interest as others couldn't buy enough.

"I hate to cook," Sara replied, spellbound by the medicinal herb concoction that Mr. Wang was creating. That was all I needed to hear. Maybe I had an edge after all. I loved to cook. I was great at it. Men loved to eat. What does Leon eat? Sara read my mind.

"We do a lot of frozen food. It's fast and easy."

It may be convenient but it all tasted pretty much the same. My mind raced. I knew now how to get to Leon. Somehow I had to cook for him.

Gus rudely pulled me out of my culinary thoughts. "Maggie, we need to leave in a few minutes or we'll be late for dinner."

For me, being redirected was unusual. On cue, Sara herded the others towards the door after a hasty but gracious thank you to Mr. Wang. No one wanted to leave.

Once people got involved in an activity, it was hard to disengage them unless something was waiting. Their chopstick lesson waited. That did the trick. Lined up outside the store, they reminded me of expected fire drills.

"Sara, two blocks down on your immediate right." Sara heard Maggie call out towards the back of the line. *Just like taking the kids to the library,* thought Sara, as she peered ahead expectantly. Just up ahead, there was a beautiful Chinese lady slowly twirling in a soft silk kimono that fluttered in the breeze. Bowing and smiling, the delicate lady ushered the hungry group into a cordoned-off room full of tables and chairs.

Sara hovered. The chairs filled up quickly. Not wanting to be concerned about what she said, Sara didn't want to sit next to a stranger. Enjoyment was what this evening was all about. As Sara hesitated, I motioned her to join us, the other tour directors and their trusty bus drivers. Separated from the significant others, we were very casual with our manners and our conversation.

As Sara sat down, I caught the surprised eye of everyone at the table. It was understood that we would all be on our best behavior. No slang and no comments about our intriguing guests. Sara blended right in. She was so interested in the other tours and what they were doing. With all the attention, the men turned giddy and seemed much more aware of their appearance than usual. Even Gus excused himself and came back with freshly combed hair and a tucked-in shirt front. Sara was a burst of spontaneous energy, from the other side. The side we all tried so hard to cater to, our clients. Our table didn't have the niceties that donned the other tables, but Sara didn't care.

Hurriedly, we passed the food and ate quickly. Since the food was an adventure in itself, Sara wanted to try everything. Never before had Sara talked with three bus drivers and numerous tour directors at the same time. Vivid imagery, intense stories, filled with mishaps and rough times. With winding supplications, it was a vivid soap opera.

They all seemed to yearn for decent relationships that their time and schedule didn't permit. To survive, they had to be vagabonds. Physically and mentally, the road kidnapped them. Sara was so glad that she chose when and where she spent time on a bus or in a hotel.

Checking my elderly clients, everyone enjoyed getting reacquainted with the chopsticks. Plates were full and plum wine was ordered by the glassful. One glass of wine was allotted per customer. A second glass was purchased. Sometimes they ordered a bottle but plum wine was sweet and caustic. It could easily dull not only your senses but your legs and arms.

When touring through a Chinese neighborhood saturated with plum wine, appearances can quickly change. Footing can be tricky. Like gossiping women, the storefronts were huddled together. Under Chinese characters that peered down from brightly colored hand-painted signs, trodden paths weaved in and out. Beside the doorways, flags fluttered revealing tiny windowpanes, which begged you to look in. There were long sticks with colorful streamers that hung inside the shops. Jade animals with glassy eyes looked back at you.

One of the shop's doors was ajar and we peered inside. A small Chinese lad, Wang Yeng, quickly appeared motioning us to come in. It was quite unusual because most of the stores had closed up hours ago. The boy's tiny hands were full of a nutty candy with sesame seeds which he offered to us. It was sweeter than the plum wine and settled the evening's meal.

An elderly man soon appeared and offered us cups of green tea, which he had been brewing in the back of the store. He spoke in bits of English, but his eyes twinkled in Chinese. Kites were everywhere. He was proud of every one of them. Box kites, animal-shaped kites with long streamers and circular kites cast their spells. There must have been something in the green tea because everyone wanted one of those kites. We could fly them once we got to the pond.

It was so welcomed when a non-scheduled event just happened. Tourists loved authenticity. Sara's eyes widened as Wang Yeng reached for her hand leading her to the back of the store by the warmed teapot. There was a little chair by a larger chair and a table with a worn book.

Sara opened the book and stared at the Chinese characters. She wanted so to be able to read them. Wang Yeng started to translate to her in English. Her heart melted. She wanted to help him so that he could buy more of those books, maybe a beginner book in English.

Sara dug deep in her pockets and found among other things the unwrapped mashed fortune cookie from dinner. Pulling the message out of the crumpled cookie, she noticed that on one side it was full of Chinese characters and the other in English. She handed Wang Yeng the fortune cookie, but regretted it when his brown eyes widened with fear. The scrap of paper slipped through his tiny fingers and fell on the floor. Reluctantly, Sara scooped up the fortune cookie and her eyes locked onto "You may not be safe, beware." Sara crumbled up the fortune cookie and tried to calm Wang Yeng, but he quickly disappeared and hung on to his father's leg for dear life.

Sara wasn't superstitious but never heard of a fortune cookie bearing bad news. She didn't believe in fortunes and especially not this one. But she did believe in staying with the group. She certainly didn't want to be left behind, not now. Mr. Yeng muttered something in Chinese as she left and wouldn't even look at her. Just minutes before, he seemed so friendly. Sara brushed it aside and hurried to catch up with the group.

"Sara, is everything all right?" I noticed she had lingered in the store a bit longer than the others.

"Wang Yeng impressed me with his English," volunteered Sara not wanting to reveal the past five minutes to Maggie or anyone else. The ceremonial custom of lighting the lantern boats intrigued Sara; wishes were for birthdays, but tonight was an exception. Glowing specs in the darkness, little lights appeared.

"We'll be stopping just up ahead to light the lantern boats. You may choose your boat." The pace quickened. The green tea had been activated. There was something infectious about a group's energy. One by one tiny candles were lit.

"Remember according to Chinese custom, wishes do indeed come true." I often wondered what happened to all the wishes. But I knew the wishers made them. They would tell me. More often than not, it was about relationships what worked and what didn't. I listened but never commented. I was not the one to give advice about relationships. Usually I wished for a good ending to the trip and that my clients would appreciate all that I tried to do for them. The tips literally helped me survive. Some were more generous than others but every little bit helped.

As I watched the boat lanterns float softly on the night water, I wondered about my kids. In the coattails of my mind, I tried my best to model for them what was and what wasn't important in life.

Right now, I needed to find Gus and the bus. Gus was right where he was supposed to be with the cleaned-out bus. Someone had trampled mud onto the floorboards and it smelled like a swamp. Now it smelled like a garden with windows that sparkled. The night lights squinted through.

After the brief tour, everyone looked spent and just wanted to retire. It didn't matter how great the outing, returning made the evening complete.

Sara couldn't wait to tell Leon what he missed. As soon as she walked into the hotel, she was sidetracked. The group was waiting for her. With drink in hand, Ariel and Dotty waved to her. A nightcap was in order.

Tomorrow they were heading back to Vancouver. Leon reminded Sara to stop at an ATM machine, so he could leave Maggie a well-deserved tip. Sara forgot. The ATM should be easy enough to find now that Gerard volunteered himself for the mission. Calling it a night, Ariel and Dotty easily declined.

It was Gerard's moment. Sara finally needed him for something. She wasn't familiar with the ATM machines since she rarely used one. Earlier,

Gerard toured the town on foot and knew where the machines would probably be. He made sure that they headed in the opposite direction. His legs suddenly became energized, and he was ready for a long hike to nowhere.

"Sara, I think there were some banks down in this direction." It was cooler and Sara was chilled. Without a word, Gerard removed his oversized jacket and wrapped it around her shoulders. Gerard just knew. He probably knew everything that Sara didn't know. She didn't know what to make of him except that he was intelligent, a gentleman, and engaged to a professional chiropractor.

Gerard had a tendency to catch her when her guard was down. Now it was nowhere to be found. Sara gulped down a bit of Victorian air and decided to enjoy the hike. It wasn't as if they were holding hands or anything. She breathed a sigh of relief and tucked her hands deep inside the coat pockets. Sara never realized that Victoria was so hilly. Her aching legs felt the incline. Sara thought that she was in good shape. This nightly hike proved otherwise. Gerard slowed down.

After about thirty minutes, a tiny restaurant loomed ahead tucked neatly away from prying eyes. Both their tired eyes saw it.

"Sara, let's stop for a cup of coffee, maybe one topped off with Irish rum. That should warm us up."

Sara couldn't wait to sit down then wished she hadn't. It was one thing to be around seventy-year olds but quite another to be around twenty-year olds. Now she felt seventy.

Focused on Gerard, the other faces slowly faded into the background.

"Sara, I remember you told me about your music. Would you like to join an orchestra someday, I mean once you really get good on your violin?"

"I never really thought about it. I was in a band once in seventh grade, and I didn't like the experience of being in a musical group. I attempted to play the drums and when I say I attempted I really did. I never took lessons and was always offbeat. One time the band director, who was once a colonel in the army, stopped the whole band and started yelling at me at the top of his military voice. I was so scared that I dropped my offbeat drumsticks. I was just a kid, not very tall, and he on the other hand was a six-foot-six giant. It was the last time I played in his band. I quit that very day. I can still hear him if I listen."

"Don't listen."

"My music steadies me but so does my family. When Leon and I have disagreements, I sometimes use my parents as a sounding board. I'm never surprised when they side with Leon, since he's usually right. They help me readjust my stubbornness making me easier to live with." What proceeded out of Sara's mouth intrigued Gerard all the more.

"You really don't look very old," said Sara, gazing at Gerard's receding hairline.

"Even without the cap?" Gerard asked imploringly. Sara was keenly aware of how men felt about losing their locks. Leon had tried various lotions to thicken his hair but few worked if at all. Hair wasn't important to Sara. What was under the hair really mattered.

"A face really tells it all. Your high cheekbones have an interesting history, I'm sure."

Gerard wondered if Sara really meant what she was saying or was just being nice. The compliment fueled his confidence.

"I guess I could say the same about you. You don't have a bunch of pretensions buried under a bunch of makeup."

Sara changed course. "Your family must be proud of you working for the government and all."

"They really don't care. They just want me to be happy doing something that I love. I just love the numbers, making it all work. Working it this way and that; checking and rechecking various money allotments."

"Do you have the final say when it comes right down to it?" Sara wondered if Gerard had to answer to anyone like she did at school.

"I do have someone to answer to, it might surprise you, but I meet monthly with him—the president and his counsel to discuss our financial course. *How exciting*, Sara thought. At school, she met with the principal once a month for department meetings, but it paled in comparison.

Loving to perform, Gerard spied a piano hovering in the corner and sauntered over towards it. He suddenly knew now how to endear himself to Sara, at least it was worth a try. A beautiful Irish ballad poured out of him. Sara melted. Passion opened her heart and charged ahead. Like a lifted veil, she saw into Gerard's soul.

Faltering, Sara considered that Gerard had something she needed. She felt an odd sense of pride when he rejoined her after his commanding debut.

"It's all in the fingers," Gerard mused as he reached for Sara's hand. Much to his surprise, it wasn't yanked away. "My fingers are just a little bit longer than yours," he quipped as he slowly measured Sara's fingers making the most of the moment. Detached, Sara gazed at him intently. Gerard's face slowly moved towards Sara's.

Sara was warmed up and ready to go. It had been an hour since they left the hotel lobby and they still hadn't found an ATM machine.

"I don't suppose that they have an ATM machine in here. It would be the perfect place with all of the college kids."

Gerard couldn't believe his surprised ears. Getting any kind of heartfelt affection from Sara was going to take a Victorian miracle. But he was far from giving up. Teachers were known for their patience but so was he. His time was running out. Tomorrow they would board the ferry then bid farewell once they arrived back in Vancouver.

More than anything, Gerard wanted a number where he could reach Sara. The attraction he felt for Sara was too disturbing to forget.

"Let's walk down the block a way and see what we can find." Sara wondered how many more blocks there were. Around the corner, there it was––a gleaming ATM machine. Unfortunately as they approached, there was an Out of Order sign on it. Sara couldn't believe it. But just up ahead there was another ATM machine that wanted business.

Gerard volunteered to input the numbers. Sara hesitated in giving Gerard their personal information. It was too cold and too late for privacy. For some unknown reason, all attempts were blocked. The machine refused to relinquish any cash. Sara lost her patience.

"I just don't understand why the machine won't accept the numbers."

"Sara, don't worry. There must be others."

Two more machines refused the bank account number. Sara felt the creeping suspicion.

"Sara, are you sure that this is the right account number?" Gerard was frustrated. He wanted to help but the numbers just didn't add up.

"Why don't I just take some money out of my account and you can pay me back later?" suggested Gerard.

He would have given Sara any amount that she wanted. Embarrassed, Sara cringed at the thought.

Rushed, Leon probably gave her the wrong account number. A mounted clock on one of the church's steeples caught her eye. It was very late, too late for excuses. Sara prayed that Leon was already asleep and not waiting up for her. She couldn't have been more mistaken.

Sara pointed to the clock. Gerard knew it was late, but figured Sara was independent and Leon let her do what she wanted to do. They were on a mission, his selfish mission. If Sara were his, she wouldn't be strolling anywhere with anyone at this hour of the Victorian night. When they finally approached the hotel, Sara's stomach was fully knotted. Being out this late with another man was catastrophic.

Thirteen years was a long time, too long to begin any new routines. Consequences waited. Once inside the hotel lobby, a lingering chill filled the air. Sara sensed what was coming and would have given anything to avoid it. Leon's temper was not to be played with.

"Sara, let me walk you up to your room," offered Gerard. Worry completely altered her face. Maybe she wasn't as independent as Gerard thought. As Sara knocked, a fully dressed Leon answered the door. Gerard chatted nervously but couldn't wait to leave.

Leon's piercing looks didn't need commentary. Sara didn't want Gerard to leave. Once he did, all sanity vanished. Accusations flew across the room like snow geese assaulting the sunset's horizon on a winter's evening. All Sara heard was something about the money and where was his dinner.

Sara needed to get out of that room. Leon's anger held her. His weakened heart might not take the added stress. Food would calm him down. It was too late for room service but she remembered seeing a fast-food restaurant across the street.

Leon was starving and angry. He didn't like the look on Gerard's face when he opened the door. When it came to his wife, there were no secrets. Since Gerard worked for the government, Leon knew that he was a smooth talker. Trust really wasn't the issue. It was late and Sara had no business being alone with anyone at this hour.

Headed for the convenience store across the street, Sara left quickly. In front of the store lingered young adolescents who wanted a hand-out. Sara shuddered knowing full well that at any moment, she might be joining them. Her bags were stuffed with everything that Leon loved. When Sara returned, Leon snored erratically. She didn't wake him up.

FERRY TO NOWHERE

||||||||||||||||||||||||||||||||||||||||||||||||||||||||||||||||||||||||||||||||||||||||||||||||||||||||||||||||||||||

S omething was visibly wrong with Sara and Leon. Well, with the whole group for that matter. No one seemed anxious to return to Vancouver since that meant everyone would be going their separate ways. Even Gus seemed reluctant to leave the island. There is something about Victoria––its charm, its charisma that fastens on to you and doesn't let you go. But we had to make the ferry in plenty of time, so I hurried the stragglers along.

I couldn't check the rooms out until everyone was down in the lobby and luggage was accounted for. Dotty and Ariel seemed exhausted and Gerard wore sunglasses with his hat pulled down further than usual. While waiting to board the bus, there was no conversation. Was my group switched?

Now was not the time for negativity, right before the finish line. It was important to have a strong finish for the trip. Champagne would lighten the mood. So I ordered a few bottles of the soothing liquid and a few cartons of orange juice. I served Mimosas on the way to the ferry. I got my group back. Well, most of them anyway. Sara and Leon were sitting further apart then usual and neither looked very pleased about anything. I needed to investigate.

"Leon, was your room to your liking?"

"Yes, there was plenty of room for me to roam around. I just didn't get much of a restful sleep. You know how it goes."

Yes, I did. As a tour director, you have to be ready to have your sleep interrupted at any hour of the night. I have taught myself to wake up abruptly and to be ready for anything. Sara turned toward me.

"It must have been something that I ate last night. I'm not myself today."

Gerard must have eaten the same food since he refused a Mimosa and didn't even have his binoculars out. Maybe the restaurant had served something that wasn't up to standard.

No doubt it would be mentioned on the evaluation forms. I just hoped that no one got sick on the ferry. Three hours on the water in a moving vehicle is no fun at all if you aren't feeling well. Gus gave me one of his inquiring looks, and I realized that I hadn't reviewed the ferry guidelines yet.

"Once we get to the loading dock, the bus will be escorted to its holding pen so to speak. Make sure before you leave the bus, you know exactly where you are so that you'll be able to find your way back to the bus. Once we arrive in Vancouver, you'll be expected to be in your assigned seats ready to leave. There are other tours here, each with their own bus so make sure you get on bus thirty-eight.

"On the ferry, you'll have access to an elevator that will take you to four different decks where you'll find restaurants and shops. It would be a great time to buy some souvenirs."

I tried to give the ferry as much business as possible. Their group rates were unbeatable. "On the upper deck, you can view waterfowl, whales, and other sea life in their natural habitat."

After all these years of returning on this same ferry, I wondered what was wrong: a knotted pain in my stomach. I could do this blindfolded with or without Gus's help. I refocused on the landing dock. Gus made good time and we were right on schedule. If you weren't on time, you missed the ferry. It waited for no one.

The first buses got the best spots in the holding area, the closest ones to the elevator. Accessibility was my major concern. Aware of Leon's difficulty with walking, I knew Gus would assist him to the elevator. There were some other elderly people on the tour who needed help as well.

Without delay, Gus ushered the bus into its designated spot and the voyagers piled out; Sara and Leon lingered behind. At least they now talked. Gerard was in no hurry and stayed behind as well. Leon was shocked when Gerard appeared at his side trying to help him. Didn't he get the message?

"About last night, I wanted to make sure that there were no misunderstandings. You might want to check that account number because it sure wasn't cooperating." Leon softened. Grudges didn't become him. He thought it through and really wasn't upset with Gerard or even Sara. Leon was very protective of Sara. Sometimes he didn't show it. Her independence clashed with his caring.

"Sara mentioned that the account numbers were wrong. Maybe it wasn't the correct sequence." Leon was back in control and wanted Gerard to know that alone time with his wife would not happen again. Gerard listened to the words "correct sequence," and felt the direct hit; Gerard's fantasies split apart. His thoughts gnawed at him. Right now, all that he wanted was to salvage his friendship with Leon. Sara wouldn't even look at him. He didn't care. He had his sunglasses on. He wasn't going to parade his thoughts in front of either of them.

Gerard just wanted to help Leon who hobbled on his crutches. Concerned, Sara wondered about their conversation. Last night's outing was erased from her thoughts. After all, she would never see Gerard again so whatever did or didn't happen didn't matter. "Passing ships in the night," as her mother would say.

Before she knew it, Sara reached the upper deck. As if playing a game with no rules, the brown pelicans bobbed up and down on debris and disappeared as the waves covered them. Rules controlled Leon. Sara hated rules. Maybe that was why she stayed out so late last night with someone she barely knew.

Gerard herded Leon towards the elevator as they made their way to the second deck. Trying to catch up, Ariel and Dotty followed closely behind.

"Gerard, how did you make out last night?" asked Ariel, wondering if they had withdrawn the needed monies. Leon turned around.

"They were unsuccessful."

"We would have gone with them, but we were completely exhausted," offered Ariel, sensing that Leon was out of sorts and wanted to dispel any misunderstanding that may have occurred. Sara was impulsive. Caring for her in a fatherly way, Ariel only saw his own daughter.

Ariel and Dotty were up part of the night wondering if Sara would even be on the tour the next day. When they saw her silent figure on the bus, they were relieved. Dotty hurried ahead noticing that Sara went to the upper deck. She sensed that Sara might need someone to talk to after hearing the words behind Leon's short reply. Dotty knew that any misunderstandings on a trip could unravel a relationship. More than anything, Dotty wanted to make sure that Sara handled the evening appropriately.

"Sara, how did you make out last night?" asked Dotty, realizing that her words did not come out exactly right. Sara winced at the words. Right now, she just wanted to be alone with her pelicans. She knew Dotty was curious, probably too curious. So she indulged her and added detailed parts that never happened. Sara liked to see how people reacted to her embellishments. Admitting that it probably wasn't the most sensible thing that she had ever done, Sara reassured Dotty as if she were her own mother. Thoroughly windblown, Dotty headed down below looking for her husband.

Milling around the ferry, I saw many headed for the specialty shops. I decided to get matching T-shirts for my kids. Three weeks was a long time to be away. Sometimes a phone call just seemed to make me miss them all the more. I wondered if they really knew how much I needed them.

When their father left, I remembered their worried faces. They wondered if I would leave as well. Almost coming true, this thought haunted me.

It was my time. I found an empty deck chair and put my feet up. No sooner had I closed my eyes when I felt the jolt. The ferry heaved backwards like a bride-to-be who suddenly changed her mind. My chair tipped over spilling me on the deck. I wasn't the only one.

Everywhere I looked, darting, questioning eyes locked on to mine. It seemed that we were all being shoved in the same direction. A terrible smell blanketed the deck reminding me of a cookout gone terribly wrong. Then I took a big, oily gulp.

Apparently something rammed itself into the ferry, or the ferry rammed into something. I was wrong on both counts. As I pulled myself up to the railing, I couldn't believe what was partly submerged in front of me, one car then another playing water tag. Panic flooded me. I felt the deck moving downward. Too many cars, too many buses, too many tour groups. The ferry had given up. Too much was expected of it. Sheer weight overcame it.

Suddenly, I remembered the gut-wrenching pain that shook me earlier today. I should have listened more closely. The others...the group...instinct rushed in. Personal items were strewn everywhere. Arms and legs were flung randomly into the air. They were hard to recognize. A steady hand somehow landed on my unsteady shoulder. It was Gerard. His radar was in control. I needed some of it.

"Maggie, we can do this together." Those six simple words connected to my weariness. "Many of the others are huddled together down by the bow near the anchor winch. The ferry is slowly taking on water so there's time."

Time for what? I thought. Didn't Gerard realize just how cold that water was? I blocked that frigid thought.

"The calmer everyone is, the better," I managed to get out, hoping that Gerard was not reading my mind. Then I heard the cry––muffled, covered, and soft. A small terrified hand reached frantically for mine. A young boy had been casually tossed between two seats and was peering out from under a blanket. My uncertainty vanished. I only saw my own terrified son peering out from underneath that blanket. How many outstretched hands were there? I had to find them.

Gerard was a cowboy who rounded up the others. Fallen figures needed to be sorted out. I guess I was more familiar with the arms and legs than I thought. As soon as I helped one person up, the favor was returned. It was contagious. Quickly, everyone was in an upright position. That was the least of our worries. The deck was not handling the water. Time was our most valuable possession. Glimpses of terror peered through the numbness. There was a blur of orange as the ferry captain commanded everyone to anchor themselves to a life preserver. My earlier-compelling thought of leaving my kids alone reawoke. I shut it down.

Leon flashed through my mind. Cool and collected as he was, I was certain Sara left him alone. Behind the first row of seats, a raised crutch rose slowly. It was attached to Leon's left arm that could barely lift it up. His face was drawn and pale. Hobbling, he headed towards me.

"Maggie, it's Sara, I can't find her anywhere."

It was how he said it that saddened me. Every line on his face was etched with desperate love. Jealousy and regret choked me. I had to find her. I knew she was on the upper deck.

"Leon, I will not come back without her."

"Her birds, all she wanted was to see her birds."

"Leon, go to the bow, look for the anchor winch. Gerard and the others should be there and you'll be safe."

"Safe? Did you really mean safe?"

What I said didn't matter. There was no safety and Leon knew it.

"Sara needs to be safe." Leon's last words clung to me as I clamored up the four sets of stairwells for the upper deck.

As I passed the silent elevators, the doors were jammed open as if controlled by a powerful clutched hand. This was the very first time that I was thankful for a broken down elevator. I imagined closed doors, chilling cries, and cramped people unable to move. The light from the upper deck blinded me.

Among the debris, there were scattered people. Sara was one of them. She looked right through me as if I were a mirage. Wincing, she grabbed her throbbing leg trying to stand up. Her pant leg was torn and matted. Wrapping my arm around Sara's waist, I gently raised her up. Shock concealed her.

"Sara, we're going to get out of this together. You're hurt. Lean on me. Give me all your weight. Remember how I was able to maneuver Leon around in his wheelchair at Butchart Gardens?"

Sara stopped shaking. Leon——that name meant something. She knew that name, she loved that name, where was that name? It all started to come back: the jolt, the fall, the blankness, their anniversary gift to Canada, the bus tour, this lady, this energy, Maggie, it was Maggie.

Sara collapsed into my *ready* arms, and I felt the weight lift off of her. Sara's color was slowly returning, and I knew she just needed some time to sorry I was wrong herself. But we didn't have that time. It would be safer below. As I looked around, I noticed others slowly following. I wished I could reach out and help them. But my hands were full. Smiling weakly, they tried to understand.

Dazed, I looked ahead of me. Without warning, the stairs jammed, spilling over with fugitives. Almost on top of one another, they tried frantically to reach the upper deck. Gerard was sandwiched in the middle, doing his best to keep some kind of order but instinct ruled. Manners were abandoned.

"Maggie, the lower deck is taking on water and splitting apart. This is our only option if we even have one."

Gerard stopped suddenly as he realized the slumped-over figure was Sara.

"Let me take her, Maggie." His strong outstretched arms cradled her. Then and there, Gerard promised himself that he and Sara were going to make it. He no longer wanted his old life. He had a new life. Time no longer controlled him. His love was no longer going to be measured by what he did or didn't do. He had found something unexpected. He felt something. He wouldn't lose it. As Gerard's thoughts rammed against him, Sara whispered "Leon." Truth rushed in quicker than the flooding ferry.

"Gerard, I can take care of her," an exhausted, hushed voice said. Both of Leon's legs completely gave up, but it didn't matter. Sara hadn't given up. She leaned against him. Leon no longer felt the knifelike pain in his stump. Even from the very first moments of his married life at the wedding ceremony, Leon's consuming pain tried to separate them. It didn't win then. It didn't win now. But the days of pain had devoured their love and created a deep, distant valley. Leon didn't know if he could get across it. He didn't fight hard enough, long enough. He gave up. When Sara touched his beaten fingers then he knew. He knew that he would fight for what they once had, a soul love that knitted them together with stitched golden cords.

"Sara, I'm so sorry. I'm sorry for everything. I'm sorry for what I haven't done, what I haven't been. Just know that when we get off this ferry, the man that holds you will be the man that you have been searching for. He'll never get lost again."

Sara heard the words that she thought she would never hear. They seemed so faraway. Were they too faraway? Did she have the strength to hold onto them? She remembered that man; the way he laughed, cried, shared, and loved. Leon pulled Sara closer to him. She felt the warmth of his body. She was very cold, too cold. Leon removed his heavy sweater and wrapped Sara in it as if she were a child.

As I looked at Leon and Sara that lump in my throat came back. But this time, I was relieved. There was no regret. My intrigue with the professor ended as quickly as it started. I had a life. It mattered to me. Whatever I did or didn't have was mine, I would live it. The only thing that this ferry was going to take away from me was my emotional baggage.

"Maggie, the captain has given the order to lower the lifeboats," Gus' anguished face paled.

Gus noticed the extra buses, the extra tours, but he didn't question, didn't ask. He should have asked. He always checked. It defined him. Why hadn't he? If only one person had. Reality grabbed him. This was his life, the bus, the ferries, the tours. It was what he knew. She was what he knew. He never told her. "Maggie, I wanted you to know how great it has been touring with you. Your "good mornings," your confident smiles, your habits, the way you carefully rummage through the daily credit card receipts, checking the itinerary, keeping us on schedule, making sure that everyone is enjoying everything...I just––"

"Gus, it isn't over. How many tours have we done together? The mishaps, remember when the bus broke down in the middle of the night and we had to wait in the freezing cold for a few hours before help came? The time when we ran out of gas when the odometer broke? This is just another one of those mishaps, but on water." It wasn't. I knew it. Gus knew it. "Let's just get everyone off this ferry."

Everyone was not going to get off this ferry. Many were in their sixties and not in the best of shape. But in the water, extra weight would insulate against the frigid cold.

Soft voices echoed one another. First one prayer, then another could be heard among the fear. Lydia, the faith healer, comforted empty hands. One hand clasped another. On the starboard side of the deck, the captain's determined hands lowered a group of bewildered teenagers into waiting lifeboats. There was an invisible sign that read: Youngest First. It was not heeded by all. Defiance showed its ugly face. Opinions were not tolerated by the captain. Next older women were helped aboard. I was thankful that I didn't have to decide who was ushered into safety.

"Maggie, this was not exactly the way we had envisioned ending our honeymoon," two cast-down voices whispered. The Israeli couple no longer gazed into one another's eyes. Their gaze focused on the invading water. I needed to say something, something that made sense. But I couldn't find the words. What could I possibly say to a newlywed couple who was just beginning to see, hear, taste, and smell joyous possibility? It wasn't fair. There was no fair.

I heard a persuasive, familiar voice behind me. Ariel's stance supported his words.

"There have been many a time on my farm when I thought it was all over, but Dotty and I survived. It's the human spirit. It dictates the outcome."

Dotty caressed Ariel's weathered hand in hers. Pride burst in Dotty. Ariel was a good man. Since his bypass surgery, Dotty was so accustomed to taking care of him that she had forgotten how much she needed him.

One widow looked to the other then back to the other. The three Australian widows were no longer anchored to their past. They no longer needed their sorrow, their loneliness, and their old way of life. Newly found freedom was in everyday. No longer would they react to life. Life would react to them. That meant getting off the flooded ferry. Their thoughts collided.

"We can do this. Death has already saturated us by taking away our husbands. What was a little ocean water?"

Their arms fastened around one another. Somehow their deceased husbands knew. Their arms were there, warm, caring, strong arms that held them. Confidence rushed in.

"We can all swim. Our families are waiting for us. We'll be on that plane. We'll step off that plane. We'll see our kids again," the Japanese couple yelled out.

The Japanese couple faced nature's wrath before. A flood nearly ended their lives. They knew water. What to expect, how to react, how cold it could be. The uncertainty had to be controlled. The time that the ferry had, the time that would elapse before help arrived—it was all about time. Mentally, they were already home. Their rock water garden splashed with reflected sunlight. Their six-year-old son ran towards them with open arms. He never left their arms.

Groups of tourists huddled together with their designated tour director. It was the last thing that I wanted to be right now. You could touch the fear, hear the frantic. The water was no longer toe-deep, but ankle-deep. Nothing would stop it. Helpless cries surrounded me. There was a cry that rose above the others.

"Maggie, the captain has radioed for help. There must be other ferries in the area, which have room for us. There's a logical way out of this. I just made some phone calls, but not even with my credentials...there just isn't enough time."

Defeat blocked Gerard. His certainty vanished. He no longer knew if he would make it.

I never saw this side of Gerard. He worked for the federal government. He always knew what to do, what to say. I thought he was a spy. I knew that he wasn't. They would save a spy. My paranoid feelings toward Gerard drowned in the knee-deep water.

Other feelings surfaced. Just before I left for this trip, my daughter pleaded with me not to go. The two weeks away from them were getting harder and harder. Why couldn't I get a job closer to home? It was me that they wanted, nothing else. Why didn't I listen? Why didn't I try? I always thought that there would be plenty of time. There was no time. Their voices, I just had to hear their voices. The low battery light on my cell phone jumped out at me. There would be no phone call. With my heart, I spoke to my kids. I thanked them for making me who I was, their mom. I thanked them for their lives, hugs, kisses, strength, and patient love. I begged God to take care of my precious children. Whatever happened on or off this ferry, it would be my last trip.

"Tighten your life preservers," was all that I could hear in between the rushing of the water. The captain was doing his best to maintain control. It was pointless. The sinking ferry was beyond his reach. The wind picked up slamming the waves against the deck. My stomach revolted. I wanted to get sick. I grabbed on to a piling beside me. It was the only thing that wasn't moving. Others grabbed on. Voices called out.

"I can't swim. The freezing water, I can't make it. I'm too old." Then I heard, "It doesn't matter."

Anger tore at me. It did matter. All of it mattered. It would take more than freezing water to stop me. Someone had yanked out pieces of discarded rope from underneath unnoticed debris in the corner. Fingers worked in unison, knotting the ropes together. No one would be swept away without consent. But they were. The waves were indiscriminate. They picked up whatever they could and pulled it down. I grabbed on some of the ropes and started making bowlines, attaching life preservers to the stretched ropes. Tough, sun-drenched farmer hands reached in to help.

"Maggie, like this," Ariel knew his knots. "This is bigger than you or me. It's bigger than any of us. It just happened. It isn't anyone's fault. It didn't happen because you brought us on this ferry."

Ariel must have read my mine. I blamed myself. He pulled harder on the rope. His words washed through me. One at a time, we formed a lifeline. The rope offered no certainty. I offered no certainty. None of us did. Around me, other tour directors panicked. The ferry had stolen our confidence. A sudden gush of water pulled at me. I didn't have time to attach myself to the lifeline. I was washed to the other side of the boat. Leon's left arm reached out and stopped me. His other arm was draped around Sara who was bent over but conscious.

"Can you hear me, Maggie? Leon's leg, I think it floats." I was sure that I hadn't heard Sara correctly. The water affected my hearing. Leon cleared his throat.

"It isn't certain but if we sink hopefully my leg won't."

The wind interrupted Leon. It had formed a pack with the waves. Wood from the deck was lifted and hurled in all directions. Gerard got slammed in the head and blood trickled down his face. He tasted blood. His eyes glazed over. If this were the end, he didn't want to go down with strangers. He cared too much. He needed too much. He crawled toward Leon and collapsed a few yards away. Within a minute, the ferry lurched ahead and water gushed like a broken fountain.

"Help me," echoed through the air.

Dotty's knees desperately tried to reach her struggling husband who was almost washed overboard. Ariel was half-submerged hanging over the side of the deck. Catching a tossed rope, he managed to hoist himself up like an unfurled flag. The flag was damaged. He could hardly stand. He only wanted to help others. He could no longer help himself. Dotty wrapped her soggy arms around her battered husband. She persuaded her knees to support her. She knew that one more wave would topple them.

Sara reached for me with her free hand. She couldn't keep Leon's secret to herself any longer. She had to tell.

"Maggie, it's Leon. He doesn't know. He doesn't know how to swim. He never learned."

Leon overheard. He wouldn't look at me. He didn't want anyone's pity. He didn't need anyone's pity. He didn't want to hear the words that just came out of Sara's mouth. She wasn't supposed to tell. She promised not to tell. Fear told.

"I just never learned. I never seemed to have the time."

"Leon, I'm an advanced swimmer and have lifeguard training. You'll not be alone in the water."

I needed him to believe me. I didn't want Leon or Sara to panic. Abruptly, the deck gave way. I panicked. Secrets were flooded. The swirling water tossed me to and fro like a beach ball. One minute I felt the deck's boards securely underneath me, the next minute there was nothing underneath my feet. Everything was numbed except my mind. Where was Leon? There were only faint outlines of those around me. Orange bobbed everywhere. It covered up faces. Leon's voice called out.

"The ferry, it's gone."

Swimming towards him, I reached his side propping him up. Sara hung on to his arm. Luckily, we were flung far enough away from the ferry so that the undertow didn't pull us down. We were orange buoys without permission. Some of the buoys swam. Some treaded water. Some floated. My ears were saturated with cries; persistent, pleading cries. Each one of us had to endure the fear, the cold, and the time. The water waited for casualties.

Gerard's floating figure came into view. He was hurt. With him were Dotty and Ariel who tied themselves together. Ariel was weakening. No one needed to tell me that help needed to come soon. I challenged what I saw. These bobbing life preservers would make it.

This was a vacation, a tour, a time to relax. It was not a time to die. Minutes ago, the captain radioed for help. Others knew. Other ferries were in the area. They would make room. There had to be room. People cared. We would be rescued.

"Keep kicking, keep your arms and legs moving. The more you move, the warmer you will be," the captain shouted.

He was in charge, but of what was in the water instead of what was on the water. I winced at the word warmer. There was no warm. Arms were everywhere, slashing through the water or locked tightly holding onto anything or anyone. Legs followed suit, kicking and treading water. Being overweight was an advantage. Extra pounds meant extra insulation and extra energy. For once in my life, I was thankful for the pounds that I was never able to lose.

"Make sure the person next to you is moving," the captain persisted.

We moved in one direction or another. The waves' rhythm had changed. The waves were getting larger with more lapsed time in between them. I made sure that Sara and Leon were ready for the swallowing waves that spit us out randomly. Leon's lips turned a slight cold light blue hue.

"My leg, it came off. The last wave tore it from my stump."

Leon ripped his waterlogged pant leg and his leg popped out. It startled me to see Leon's leg floating without him. There was enough room for the three of us to hold on. White wrinkled fingers appeared out of nowhere. Ariel and Dotty attempted to grab on. There wasn't any room. I let go. Moaning, Gerard fastened himself on to Leon's available floating foot. The cold permeated every pore. My body didn't listen to my slowed mind. I imagined things. Outstretched arms reached up to heaven. My mind snapped.

Then I heard it, the sound of whirling propellers. Peering up, I saw a flock of mechanical geese. Helicopters, branded with federal markings followed one another in line formation. Dangling from their midsections were suspended ropes with swinging wire baskets. I knew it. Gerard was a spy. A spy was on my bus. Shadowy figures camouflaged in black wet suits slowly lowered themselves. One by one, the baskets hit the water. The wet suits plunged into the waves. It was a spy thriller without the music. Professional arms took over. Struggling bodies wrapped in orange were lifted into the moving baskets. I thought it was indiscriminate but it wasn't. I was sure that luck had something to do with it, but it didn't. The wet suits rescued the older people first. Hair color was the radar. Mine was dark brown, so I would have to wait.

Gerard couldn't wait. Gerard's face was nearly ashen. He no longer held onto Leon's foot. He had to get into one of those baskets. A spy had to be rescued. Weakly, I lifted my arms and tried to wave them back and forth. They didn't want to move. I didn't stop. Just when I thought my aching arms hadn't been successful, a steady arm reached under Gerard's limp body and guided him into a basket. One of my frozen prayers had been answered.

When the wet suit returned, he hesitated then dove repeatedly under the waves searching frantically. There wasn't anyone else in our immediate area. I couldn't figure out who he was looking for.

Ariel watched, realizing what he was doing. He yelled out, "The leg doesn't belong to anyone. It's prosthesis."

A look of sheer relief covered the diver's face. As he approached Ariel, he pinched the leg to make sure. Dotty wouldn't let go of Ariel.

"Take her first," his love commanded. Dotty didn't resist. Her fight was gone. Her knees gave up long ago. I watched love have its way. As I watched Dotty being hoisted up, I knew that time was against us. There were just too many to save. There would not be a basket for me. Within minutes, it was Ariel's turn or so I thought.

"Leon, you're next," quipped Ariel.

"Ariel, it isn't going to happen that way. You belong with your wife. She can't make it without you." Leon had a deep respect for their love. It was a love that you didn't often see. He felt privileged to witness it. Throughout the trip, Leon developed a heartfelt connection with Ariel. He reminded him of his own father. It was a connection that he wouldn't risk losing. Leon made sure that Ariel was safely secured in the basket. Then he gave me a long stare. He knew.

"Maggie, I just don't think...there just isn't..."

He didn't finish his sentence. Sara was listening. He refused to drown her hope. Sara couldn't focus clearly.

"Leon, your face, I can't see your face."

"I'm right here. If you need to rest, close your eyes. The rope should be back any minute."

As Sara closed her eyes, Leon's eyes gave way to hot, angry tears. His wife would live. The ocean would not claim her. He wrapped his arms around her. Death would have to go through him to get to her. I wanted to say something, anything. But I didn't. Sara was drifting in and out of consciousness. I couldn't stop my own tears. I cried for me, for the man that never was beside me, for my son and daughter, for precious time that I couldn't get back. My last frozen prayer was for God's forgiveness and mercy. I wanted to go quickly and quietly. I kissed my children good-bye and allowed myself to let go. From out of nowhere appeared a mirage, the most beautiful ferry that I ever saw. It darted slowly through the waves with confidence. It was maneuvered by God himself.

"Leon, it's over."

"Maggie, there's still time. Don't give up. Maybe..."

"No, Leon, over there. They didn't forget us."

Leon had just enough energy to turn his head and see the slowing ferry. Without hesitation, orange life preservers were hauled aboard. Frozen bodies were somehow coaxed back to life. Blankets were piled relentlessly on each one of us. Continuous rubdowns and hot coffee warmed my paralyzed body. My mind began to thaw. Looking out on the water, all that I could see was blue. It was all that I needed to see. Our old lives were all that remained behind in the sea. Time had been given back to us. Bundled up, Leon still held Sara in his arms, blankets and all. He looked at me. He knew.

The raging waves of the sea swept away the brokenness. Each one of us was given another chance, to make it right.

Printed in the United States
by Bookmasters

Printed in the United States
By Bookmasters